Trapped
ALONE

Joann Herley

ACKNOWLEDGEMENTS

Cover Photos by:
© Volodymyr Byrdyak | Dreamstime.com
© Marinaistock | Dreamstime.com

Cover Design by: Joann Herley
Edited by: EBH and P. Maier
Formatted by: P. Maier

Dedication

To those that never gave up on love

Special Thanks

to

Ashley Hayslip

for providing a name for the Griffin
Commander

"Krega"

Pre-Production Sketches

These sketches were done by Steve Newton to help pitch the Swindlers film project to investors, production companies, filmmakers, and actors.

A look at an exasperated Bob speaking with the holographic representation of the ship's computer.

Bob gets a briefing from his crew about the asteroid.

This was the first sketch of the ship's bridge.

Books by the Author

The Evergreen Series

Book I - Seized by Obscurity
Book II - Escaping Obscurity
Book III - Protected from Obscurity
Book IV - Shattering Obscurity

* * * *

Trapped Alone - A Prequel to the
Evergreen Series
Laralynn's Turn - Coming in 2017

A Prequel to the Evergreen Series

The Love Story
of a
Warlock and his Wolf

Their Love was Always and Forever

Prologue

Needing to stop and rest, Kayleigh leaned her hand upon the rough bark of a pine tree. She was desperately trying to catch her breath and control her breathing, but a fit of ragged coughing had replaced her gentle wheezing. Hearing another snapping twig, she jerked her head toward the sound. This time, it seemed much closer. Could she hear panting, or was it only the sound of her own gasps for air that filled her ears? Nervously looking over her shoulder, she could see nothing but the movement of dark shadows within the forest. Even though she couldn't see it, she knew it was there. She could feel it watching her and waiting for the right moment to strike. It had been clever and kept itself hidden, but she knew it had been following her. It had been following her ever since she had taken her leave of Woods Village.

She had made the trip from Woods Village back home again to Fallon Castle several times but never on foot and never alone. This time, she had foolishly made the trip alone and regretted declining the assistance of a tall handsome man she had met in the village square. Even though he knew of her father, Lord Fallon, she felt that it was not proper to accept his offer. Now, she would have willingly traded the bitter words from her father for the safety of being perched in front of him on his horse.

Trying to push the fear from her mind, she headed toward the clearing that surrounded Fallon Castle. Wanting to run but knowing it would only heighten its excitement for the chase, she walked slowly toward the sun filled clearing. The castle was within sight and only a short walk to reach the safety of its wooden gate. Noticing the guard in the tower, she waved her arms to draw his attention. Seeing him wave back, she stepped from the shelter of the forest keeping her eyes on the guard.

Just keep walking, it will be afraid to follow me into the sun filled clearing, she thought.

A low steady growl made her halt. She could feel the warmth of the sun against her face, but it did nothing to calm the sudden chill of fear that possessed her body. Holding her breath and closing her eyes, she could only hear the sound of her heart pounding. She didn't know how close it had come until she felt the pain of its bite as its jaw clamped down upon her hand. She screamed as she struggled to pull her hand away from the mouth of a black wolf. Seeing the blood dripping from her fingers, she swayed for a moment before she dropped to the ground, and a dark red haze covered her vision.

"Kayleigh! Kayleigh, wake up," her mother said, as she gently shook her daughter's shoulder. "Wake up, my dear. You are having a nightmare."

Kayleigh slowly opened her eyes. Seeing worry upon her mother's face, she felt a cold shiver race down her spine. Looking about and seeing the familiarity of her bedchamber, she gradually felt her body relax. She was far from the forest, and the wolf that had followed her. Taking a moment to thank the stars, she smiled knowing it had only been a dream.

"Now that you are awake, are you hungry?" asked her mother. "Food will surely take your mind off your nightmare."

"I am famished," Kayleigh replied.

"I think a little bread and broth would be good for you," her mother said, as she headed for the door. "I will ask Mercy to bring it to your chamber."

Watching her mother leave through the open door, Kayleigh looked at the sunlight that spilled upon the stone floor through the open window. As she tried to sit up, fierce pain stung her hand and shot up her arm. Pulling her hand from beneath the bed linens, she saw a strip of linen wrapped around her palm and fingers. A tinge of red had seeped through the soft linen layers.

"What happened?" she gasped, as she began to remember her dream and started to cry. "It was real; it wasn't a dream. My stars, it was real."

Tears streamed down her face as she cradled her wounded hand against her chest. She had heard the stories and knew what it meant to be bitten by a wolf. She would be banished from the love of her family and the safety of the castle forever. The wolf would own her completely. It would own her body and her soul.

Chapter 1

Gautier leaned back against a moss covered boulder along the edge of Whistler's River. It had long been his favorite place to rest in the shade of the pine trees and ponder his future. He had suddenly become bored with his life, and he had begun to question everything about his place at Black Thistle Castle. Ever since his father had died and his brother had become the Lord and Master of Black Thistle, he had grown tired of the position of his brother's Chancellor. He was honored to have his brother lean on him for advice, but it had turned into a mindless quest of visiting the surrounding villages offering them Lord Heinrich's assistance and protection. After all, he was a warlock, and he could offer protection with a snap of his fingers.

Feeling Velsa's head resting against his chest, he took comfort in her affection and thought fondly of their first meeting. She had been his constant companion for nearly two decades and never once betrayed him. It was quite by accident that he had found her. A trip to Cobb Cove to pay for a small herd of sheep had found him gazing at her standing on the cliffs as she watched the seagulls. Purely out of curiosity, he had approached her. As she turned to face him, her flaxen braid had suddenly unraveled at her back giving the illusion of golden wings spread wide ready to take flight. At that very moment, he had wanted to know her, and they had been together from then until now.

"I could stay like this forever," Velsa whispered.

"You satisfy much too easily," Gautier replied. "However, I must return to the castle. I promised Lord Heinrich I would be back in time for the council meeting. I'm sure he has created some new assignment for me."

"Not yet," she purred, as she tucked her fingers inside the opening of his tunic.

Feeling her light touch upon his skin, he searched for the bolt of heat that would confirm she was the one intended for him. After all this time, that feeling had yet to manifest itself, and he knew he should be searching for the one that would make his life complete. Removing her hand, he stood and pulled her up into his arms. Gently placing a kiss upon her forehead, he couldn't help but worry what ending their relationship would do to her.

* * *

The full moon had proven the assumed outcome of the wound upon Kayleigh's hand, and she was informed that she must leave the castle. Even after begging her father on bended knee and seeing her mother collapse after hearing the edict, her father told her the risk to his people would be too great to allow her to stay.

Upon leaving the castle, her mother had secretly given her enough coin to ease her tearful departure. Sitting within a horse drawn cart, Kayleigh waved good-bye to her mother until the wooden gate closed leaving her alone outside the walls of the castle. Knowing that she could never return, Kayleigh slowly made her way along the worn path to Wintergreen Mountain in hopes of hiding her affliction in the bitter winter snowfall.

For almost thirteen years upon the mountain, she had been happy and successful in hiding her secret. Her new home within the forest had allowed her white wolf to run freely, and she had easily concealed her in the cold white winters. Kayleigh had finally felt the love and protection offered by her wolf and willingly returned her affection.

On one occasion, she had bravely allowed her wolf to venture through the mountains to stand near the waterfalls that overlooked Fallon Castle. A single glimpse of her mother was all that she desired. It was just before sunset that she finally saw her mother step out onto her balcony and lean against the stone railing. Upon seeing her, her wolf released a mournful howl that had caused her mother to turn her head toward the sound. Their eyes met for only a moment before her wolf turned and raced away. Fortunately for Kayleigh, it wouldn't be the last time she ventured through the mountains, and it wouldn't be the last time her mother waited for a glimpse of her daughter's wolf.

It was the continued curiosity of her continued youth by some of the women, and the whispering behind her back that finally made her leave her beloved mountain. Hoping to find a way to support herself in Shepard's Grove, Kayleigh used the last of her coins to secure a small one room cottage in the nearby forest. It was far enough away from the nearest village square for privacy but close enough for her to obtain necessities.

It was here that her mother found her in the market trading wild mushrooms and berries for eggs. She had just put her basket filled with eggs over her arm and turned to leave when she heard her mother's voice. Afraid to draw attention to herself, she made her way out the open doorway to the shade of a nearby tree to wait for her. As her mother walked toward her, she noticed the color of her hair had changed from a golden flax to grey, and her skin was very pale. She realized that time had aged her mother, unlike herself. Tears filled their eyes as they spoke for the few moments they were offered before a guard led her mother back to her carriage. In their short conversation, her mother had promised to visit her the next time she came to the village. Little did she know that her mother's surprise visit would be her last. She died not long after her visit from a bleeding cough, and the same illness took her father before the weather turned cold. Hearing the news left Kayleigh heartbroken and alone with no one to comfort her but her wolf.

Sadly, peace was short lived. Again, time proved to be her enemy. The village women felt threatened by her, and constantly asked why she did not wed, or how she stayed so young. In the dead of night, she packed up her belongings and left her cottage.

It had been well over thirty years since she had been to Woods Village. Several new buildings had been built in the seaport square, and many more people scurried from shop to shop. The waterway had been good for the village, and she hoped it would offer more possibilities for work. Not recognizing any of the village folk, she felt certain her identity would not be discovered. Her secret would finally be safe, and Kayleigh hoped to keep it that way. Needing to find a peaceful life away from questions and curiosity, she began to search for a place she could make her home.

* * *

Kayleigh sat on the wooden porch of her tiny cottage. Sitting on the edge of the cliffs beyond Woods Village, her cottage overlooked the splendor of the sea. She had spent many an early morning watching the beautiful orange or yellow glow of a sunrise, and this morning was no different. Wrapped in a woolen blanket, she sat barefoot with her knees tucked under her chin and her arms about her legs. The crisp morning breeze stung her toes and her face, but she willingly suffered through it to see the morning come to life before her. It made her feel human with those few precious moments every morning. Taking in the last of the colors reflecting upon the water, she reluctantly stood and made her way back into the warmth of her cottage.

After dressing quickly and replacing her hunger with a cup of tea and a wedge of cheese upon a slice of bread, she grabbed her shawl from the peg by the door. Securing it around her shoulders, she tossed her empty honey cup into her basket. With her basket over her arm, she began humming a familiar tune as she opened the door and headed for the village square. It was a bit of an uphill walk to the square, but she always enjoyed the way it made her heart pound. It wasn't as good as running in her wolf form, but it was good just the same. People offered their morning greetings as they quickly walked past her, and she returned their kindness with a smile.

Hearing the soft jingle of the bell as Kayleigh opened the door to Big John's Market, she smiled and made her way to the wooden counter. Big John was standing high upon the rung of his ladder with his back to her. She stood quietly waiting for him to descend. As he did, he turned to greet her with a grin.

"Madame White," he bellowed. "What brings you out this fine morning?"

Kayleigh had taken the name Kay White to try and fend off some of the curiosity. She had devised a story about a husband that spent a great deal of time at sea as part of the crew that worked the ships in the bay. She felt this would keep men seeking a wife from proposing, and the women would worry less about having their husbands stolen. So far, it had worked to her benefit. The village women had allowed and sometimes offered the supervised help of their husbands to make repairs to the rundown cottage she called home.

"I am in need of honey and a few fresh figs," she replied. "I believe that I still have enough credit for the purchase."

"Indeed you do," Big John said, as he lifted the lid of a crock that sat upon the counter. "Have you a vessel?"

Kayleigh handed him a small slender cup with a piece of linen tied about the top as she sat her basket on the counter. She watched him remove the linen and drizzle the carved wooden wand filled with the honey into the cup. The thick amber reflected the morning light from the open window making it look like liquid gold. Securing the tie, he placed it in her basket.

"The figs are in the large oval basket by the door. Take what you need."

"Thank you," Kayleigh said. "I should be back with a good batch of wild onions the day after tomorrow. I have found a small patch that offers the sweetest little morsels. I am sure you will be able to offer me a good trade."

"You haven't failed me yet," he laughed. "Good-day to you, Madame White."

"Good-day, Big John," she replied.

Kayleigh turned and headed for the basket of figs by the door. Selecting a few, she settled them securely around the cup of honey. With her errand complete, she reached for the door handle and stepped out into the bright sunlight. Trying to shield her eyes from the brightness, she carelessly took a step directly into someone's path. Feeling the pressure of someone's hands grasping her arms, she looked down to see a pair of black leather boots and up to see a neatly trimmed black beard. The sight of his dark eyes stole her breath away.

Gautier felt the woman sway as he tightened his grip to keep her from falling. As he did, he felt heat pulsing within his hands. Making sure to secure her upon her feet, he dropped his hands to his side and took in the crystal blue of her eyes.

"Excuse me, sir. The sunlight reflected in my eyes, and I did not see you," Kayleigh shyly apologized.

"It was I that stepped into your path," he replied.

Taking a step back, she lowered her face trying to hide the blush of color that she knew spread across her cheeks. Feeling a sudden nervous warmth, she pulled her shawl from her shoulders.

"I bid you a good day, sir," she said, as she stepped from the wooden porch toward the dirt path that would take her home.

"Wait," he shouted, a little too eagerly. "May I know your name?"

Wanting to ignore him but feeling the need to respond, she turned and took in his dark eyes one more time.

"My name is Kay White. You may call me Madame White," she replied.

Hearing her say her name, he knew that she was deceiving him. She was hiding something, and she was hiding it from everyone. Not wanting to embarrass her in front of the onlookers that had suddenly taken notice of their conversation, he let her precious little lie rest.

"Good day to you, Madame White," he responded.

He had felt the heat through his gloves and knew what it meant. She was the one intended for him, of that, he was certain.

I will discover your true name and soon have the pleasure of your company, he thought.

He watched her walk away from him until the sun took her from his sight. Bringing his hand to his forehead to shield his eyes, he detected a surprising scent that caused him to laugh.

"My little deceiver is also a wolf," he whispered under his breath. "What other surprises does this little wolf hide from me?"

Deciding to stay in the village to find out, he made his way to secure a room at the tavern. He wasn't about to head back to Black Thistle anytime soon.

Resting her head against the inside of her cottage door, Kayleigh rubbed her hands over her arms. She could still feel the warmth from where he had grabbed her to keep her from falling. Kayleigh knew what it meant, and she decided, then and there, to do anything she could to avoid seeing him again. She couldn't let him know about her wolf. If word got out, the people of the village would run her from her home or worse, kill her.

* * *

The full moon was approaching, and Kayleigh's wolf constantly pushed her for release. She could feel her anger, but she had forcibly kept her wolf hidden since meeting the stranger. One more day and her wolf would come forth whether she liked it or not. The full moon belonged to her wolf, and she had no right to keep it from her. They just needed to be careful.

Kayleigh walked the tunnel from her cottage to the cluster of trees that shielded the village from the bitter cold of the sea breeze. It had been a chance find when a few rotten floor boards had needed to be replaced. When she asked about the tunnel, the village men only knew of the tales told in the tavern of smugglers using a tunnel to carry stolen silver coins and weapons from Fallon Castle to the waiting ships in the harbor. It had long been forgotten, and no one knew where or if it really existed. Discovering the tunnel had collapsed, the men found the space below her cottage good for nothing more than storing tools or vegetables during the cold season. Little did they know, she had gradually cleared the tunnel and used it to hide her wolf's passage to and from the cottage.

Bending down to crawl from the hidden tunnel, Kayleigh glanced about to make sure she was alone before she moved out into the open. The sun was at its highest point in the sky, and the salty sea breeze felt good against her face. With her basket over her arm, she stepped away from the boulders that hid her secret passage and headed for the berries she knew were ripe and ready to be picked. She would fill her basket and make her way to the Old Signal Tower to see after the caretaker, Mr. Brumley.

On the way, she walked past the bell shaped blooms of the Black Nightshade grumbling to herself. It hadn't been long since she had hacked it down to the roots, but the green leafy plant full of poisonous jewel like berries had returned from the dead to mock her. She had feared that some unsuspecting child would be drawn to the bright berries, too curious to resist them, and she had tried her best to ruin them.

"Enjoy the sun while you can, for I shall return to put an end to you."

Glad that no one had heard her, she laughed as she lifted her skirt and ran through the tall sweet grass until she reached the clump of Sea-Buckthorn bushes. The branches were covered with ripe berries, and she knew they would make delicious jelly for herself and a good trade at Big John's Market.

As she carefully picked the berries trying to avoid the thorns, she thought about the stranger that grasped her arms to keep her from falling. There was something about him that made her wonder if she had seen him before. His dark mysterious eyes were beautiful but became magical when he smiled. Pricking her finger on a sharp thorn, she quickly put the wounded finger into her mouth. The sudden pain drew her back to her task at hand, and she pushed the stranger from her mind. There was no way that she could let herself get involved with anyone, least of all a handsome stranger. With her basket filled, she made her way to the narrow dirt path that led to the tower.

Halfway to the tower, she noticed a horse and rider coming toward her. With only a narrow path for them to share, she looked for a place where she could safely step aside to allow the horse to pass. It wasn't until the horse was almost upon her that she realized it held the boar and thistle markings. Stepping back into a patch of dry grass, she bowed her head and curtsied to show respect to the rider. Hearing the horse stop before her, she looked up to see the stranger looking down at her.

"Madame White, we meet again."

"Sir, you have me at a great disadvantage."

Gautier dismounted and walked around his horse letting the reins fall to the ground. As he took a step toward her, he saw her take an uneasy step back into the tall grass.

"Forgive my rudeness, Madame. My name is Gautier Heinrich."

Kayleigh gave him a slight nod and looked again at the markings.

"I believe the markings upon your horse are royal markings, are they not? Have I misspoken? Should I have addressed you as My Lord?"

"I would prefer that you address me as Gautier. I find that it results in fewer questions and much easier conversations. My brother is Lord Heinrich of Black Thistle Castle. I am, as some would call me, The Messenger."

She pursed her lips to keep from laughing, but he saw a spark of light in her blue eyes that he found intriguing.

"What brings you all the way out to Mr. Brumley's tower?" she asked.

"Big John sent me with oil for his lanterns. He does a great service to Woods Village and the ship captains by keeping them burning throughout the night. And you, what brings you this far from the village?" He eagerly awaited the sound of her voice.

"I picked a basket of berries and thought to share some with Mr. Brumley. I help with his washing and hang it to dry in the sun. He has been alone since Madame Brumley's passing and has no one to help him."

"You are a kind soul."

"He needs help, and I am able to lend a hand."

"It is a dusty path. Come, let me take you."

Before she could protest, he scooped her up and set her upon his horse. Taking hold of the reins, he easily swung his leg up over the saddle to sit behind her. Clutching her securely around her waist, he turned his horse toward the tower. Uncomfortable with their closeness, she tried to lean away from him, but his hand kept her back pressing against his chest. Warmth began to travel up her spine, across her shoulders, and down her arms as she listened to the sound of her heartbeat pounding in her ears. Even though it was loud, its rhythm seemed to soothe her. In fact, it had distracted her and kept her from hearing him call her name.

"Madame White, Madame White, we are here."

Startled, she hadn't realized her eyes had been closed and squinted at the bright sunlight.

"Mr. Brumley, I have brought you a visitor. I saw her walking toward your tower and couldn't bring myself to make her walk all this way."

Hearing someone talking, she looked down to see Mr. Brumley walking slowly toward the gate. Holding onto his walking stick with both hands, he smiled up at her. She felt Gautier release her waist before he dismounted his horse. With that sudden release, the warmth she had enjoyed disappeared and left her body feeling chilled. She watched as he took her basket and sat it down upon the stone path.

"Now, let's get you down from there."

He reached up and grasped her waist. As he lifted her from his horse, she rested her hands upon his shoulders and let them slide down his arms as he sat her feet securely on the ground.

"Thank you, it was kind of you to carry me, but I wouldn't have minded the walk."

"Why walk when I can carry you?"

She blushed as she bent down to retrieve her basket. Unlatching the gate, she quickly opened it and closed it behind her. Reaching to secure the latch, she felt Gautier place his hand over hers.

"I will return to see you safely home. There is a storm coming."

She looked out over the dark water and saw nothing but white clouds and sunshine. Searching for what he had seen, she looked back at him for an explanation, but saw only the lifting of his brow and a playful grin.

"Enjoy the berries she has brought you, Mr. Brumley, and be sure to ready your lanterns. There is a fierce storm coming. The captains will be watching for the light to guide them home."

"I can feel the hint of it in the air," replied Mr. Brumley.

"Now, go help Mr. Brumley. I will return just before the sea begins to pull the sun down into its water."

She watched him mount his horse and gallop away down the path. Confused and a bit angry with herself, she turned to see Mr. Brumley slowly heading back toward his door. Picking up the hem of her skirt, she followed him up the stone steps, but she stopped to take one last look at Gautier, her mysterious stranger, before he was gone from view.

* * *

Rain had pounded her cottage throughout the night, and she worried that the fierce wind would rip the thatching from her roof. The sound of its constant howling had granted her little sleep. When she was able to sleep, her dreams were of a mysterious faceless stranger draped in a dark cloak. It flew through the air chasing her wolf through the forest and scraping its claws over her back. Left wounded and dying in the forest, her secret was soon discovered by hunters. As they dragged her behind their horses, Kayleigh suddenly woke to the sound of her own whimpering. After waking from the same repeated nightmare, she knew it was a warning. It was a warning to protect her secret and be cautious around strangers.

With the first light of dawn starting to seep through her bedchamber window, Kayleigh decided to forgo her attempt at any further sleep. Wrapping her shawl around her shoulders, she set about starting a fire to take the chill from her small cottage. With the flames licking against the dry twigs eager to wrap themselves around a few dry logs, she opened the door to see what the morning had to offer.

The remains of a few dark clouds lingered in the sky, but the rain had finally stopped. Looking at the numerous puddles the rain had left behind, she knew her wolf's moonlit run would be muddy, and she would be in need of water for a bath. Thankfully, she had taken the time to put her buckets out to collect the rain water before she had gone to bed. Otherwise, she would've had to haul the water all the way from Woodcutter's Water, and it would have taken her all day. The likelihood of her completing that chore without seeing Gautier on the way would have been highly unlikely. Feeling the rumble of her hungry stomach, she reached for two of the buckets and made her way back inside.

* * *

From the moment he had awakened, his thoughts were of Madame White. There was no denying she was his intended mate. It took every bit of his willpower to keep from riding to her cottage and taking her in his arms. He had felt the heat race through his body as he held her against his chest, and the way she had willingly molded herself against him. He was sure that she had felt it too.

The day had passed much too slowly for Gautier, but the sun had finally given into the darkness of the night's sky. He knew the moon would be full, and she would release her wolf to run in the moonlight. He wanted to be there to see her. Throwing his cloak over his shoulders, he left his small room and headed down the stairs of the tavern. Making his way through the crowd of locals, he opened the tavern door and looked up at the bright full moon. He had never been drawn to the moon before, but he found that the sight of it took his breath away. Closing the door behind him, he hurried to the stable.

As he sat upon his horse, he started to mentally reach for her wolf, but he quickly pulled his focus back. He didn't want to scare her wolf before she had a chance to run. He didn't want to scare either one of them. Unsure of where to go, he gave his horse a quick kick with the heels of his boots and headed for the forest nearest her cottage.

The ground was thick with mud, the trees were narrowly spaced, and it offered him little room to maneuver his horse. Dismounting, he tethered him to a tree and took off on foot. After putting a good distance between himself and his horse, he noticed he had found a small clearing and looked for a place to hide. He knew she would surely catch his scent if he stayed on the ground. Looking about for a tree he could easily climb, he spotted one with low broken branches, and he laughed as he grabbed one branch after another to reach the top. He had never gone to this much trouble to see a woman or a wolf.

After waiting for what seemed like forever, he was ready to give up and make his way down the tree. Wrapping his cloak around his waist, he turned and gripped a branch while reaching for another with his foot. Finding secure footing, he began to lower himself to the ground. Midway down, he stopped. He could hear something running toward him. Afraid to move and give himself away, he quickly hid himself from view.

With mud covering her legs, he saw the white wolf leap over a downed tree and come to a sudden stop in the middle of the clearing. Her snout was in the air, and her ears flicked from side to side searching for danger. Finding none, she lowered her mouth to drink from a shallow puddle of water leftover from the rain. Her coat seemed to shimmer in the moonlight, and he longed to run his fingers through her thick fur. He flinched as the loud call of an owl above him drew her eyes up toward the bird that had invaded her privacy. Her golden eyes were mesmerizing, and he found himself being drawn in by her gaze. Not thinking, he wanted to get a closer look, and he moved his foot to find a lower branch. The unexpected noise startled her. The flick of her tail was the last he saw of her before she was hidden by the trees. Disappointed that she was gone, Gautier climbed down the tree and made his way back to his horse.

* * *

Kayleigh's wolf was careful to take a different path back to the tunnel's entrance and scented the air for danger before entering. Making her way through the tunnel to the hole in her cottage floor, she surrendered her wolf over to Kayleigh's human form. Climbing up through the flooring, she carefully placed the boards back in their proper place. Satisfied that they were secure, she picked up the blanket she had left on the floor and wrapped it around her naked body.

Every muscle in her body was sore, but the soreness felt wonderful. She had waited too long since her last run, and she would feel it tomorrow. Looking over at the bathing tub she had filled with boiling water before she left, she hoped it hadn't cooled too much. She had stayed in the forest longer than she had intended, and a cold bath would do nothing for the soreness in her arms and legs. Dipping her hand into the water, she was surprised to find it to be quite warm. Dropping the blanket, she stepped in and sat down. Letting her head rest against the edge of the tub, she closed her eyes and felt her tired body relax in the warmth of the water.

Before long, she felt the water begin to cool. Using her last bit of soap, she washed the mud from her hair and then her body. Standing she picked up the pail of water by the tub and poured it over her head. Stepping from the tub, she dried herself and pulled her sleeping gown over her head.

Not ready to climb into bed, she fed what remained of the fire and sat down by the hearth to absorb its warmth. Thinking back on her run, she remembered the old owl that had called to her. She wondered if his call had been a warning of some kind. A strange sound coming from his tree had caused her to race away.

Was it the faceless stranger from my dreams?

She laughed and pulled her knees up under her chin and wrapped her arms around her legs. Putting the silly thought out of her mind, she began to worry about Gautier and whether she would see him tomorrow. She couldn't hide in her cottage forever. She would just have to put him in his place. After all, everyone knew she had a husband.

Chapter 2

The next morning brought more disappointment when Gautier received word that he was needed back at Black Thistle Castle, and reluctantly, he had returned. Standing in the Great Hall waiting for his brother, he couldn't stop thinking about the beautiful woman that had stolen his heart with a single touch. She was more than he could have ever imagined, and he wanted to return to Woods Village to be near her. Thinking back on the day he had carried her to Old Signal Tower, his thoughts of her were suddenly interrupted with the sound of his brother's boots.

"Gautier, it is good to see you," shouted Gerwig, as he made his way toward his brother.

"Lord Heinrich," Gautier replied. "You have need of me?"

"Please, I am and always will be Gerwig to you."

"Gerwig, you have need of me?"

"I have received good news. Lord Larchmont has finally agreed to my proposal for his daughter's hand in marriage."

"I understand the need for a formal request. It is the way things are done, but has Petula agreed to this arranged marriage? Will you have a resentful bride?"

"She has agreed; however, I believe her agreement is more to appease her father's will. It is difficult to court her properly with so much distance between us."

"You intend on courting her?"

"I will not marry her if she is not pleased with me. There should be some strand of affection that binds two people together in marriage. I will not marry her if she is unwilling. That is why I have asked you to return. I need your help."

"Gerwig, I appreciate the confidence you have in me, but what can I do to make her pleased with you?"

"I am asking you to go to Featherstone Castle and escort her back to Black Thistle. I am sure she will have maidens to attend to her, but it is our responsibility to provide protection during the voyage."

"When is this voyage to take place?"

"As soon as you can ready a ship to sail to Crownnail Island."

"You know that island is thought to be inhabited by griffins? They are not particularly friendly with strangers to the island."

"That is exactly why I am sending you. What better way to defend Petula and her maidens from aggressive griffins than by sending a warlock?"

"If this woman is who you desire to be your bride, I will go make a ship ready to bring her to Alltree. When we return, I ask that you not include me in your quest for her affection."

"Brother, you wound me. I believe that I have the needed skills to charm a woman on my own. If not, she is free to return to her father. I want no conjured love potions to make her stay with me."

"We will see, brother. We will see if you can charm this innocent flower. I might even forgo my return to Woods Village to watch this spectacle."

"What's in Woods Village that has you ready to return?"

"I have discovered a white wolf. I spotted her the evening before you called me back."

"The wolf will still be there when you have finished with your current task. Now, be off with you. I am eager to see Petula and claim her affection."

Gautier left his brother and made his way toward the Command Center in search of Reginald, the Commander of the

Black Thistle Army. He needed his help in obtaining a ship and supplies for the voyage to and from Crownnail. He could certainly conjure a ship, but if the spell was broken by one of the griffins, they would all drown in the sea. Better to have a proper ship secure underfoot and fight the griffins with magic than the alternative.

Pushing the heavy door open, he looked about for the commander. Seeing a group of men hovered around a long table, he could hear Reginald's raspy voice. The commander had taken a blade to his neck during a skirmish long before he had come to Black Thistle, and his voice had suffered from the wound. He wore a thick red scar that wrapped under his chin from one ear to the other. That, along with both ears severed from his head, leant to his fierce appearance. He was stronger than most, highly skilled with a variety of weapons, and the best commander Lord Heinrich had ever had. Reginald had pledged his life to protect Black Thistle, and in return, he had earned Gautier's trust and respect.

"Commander, could I speak with you?" asked Gautier, as he approached the table.

Reginald gave a nod and dismissed the other men.

"I need your help in obtaining a ship to sail to Crownnail Island. I am to escort Lady Petula to Black Thistle. It seems Lord Heinrich has asked her father for her hand, and he has agreed."

"Do you also have an agreement with the griffins? They can be quite protective of their island."

"Hopefully, my magic will subdue them long enough for us to put a good distance between us and them."

"I will see to it. I assume you are to sail immediately?"

Gautier tapped the table with his knuckles and nodded his head.

"My brother is eager to charm her into becoming his bride. I am eager to get the chore completed."

"I can understand. I am eager to charm a lady into becoming my bride too."

"Your time will come, Reginald. Be patient, your time will come."

Reginald laughed and pointed to his neck and where his ears should be.

"With all of this, I truly doubt it. I frighten those ladies that aren't soaked with ale or need the candles snuffed out."

"I have told you; I would help you. You need only ask it of me."

Shaking his head, Reginald looked down at the stone floor.

"It is my burden to bear, and bear it, I will until I die."

"Reginald, if the time comes that you wish to abandon your current desire, I will help you. If not, I will respect your decision."

"My Lord, I thank you for your gracious offer. Now, let me get to work on obtaining you a ship. I will also send a few from the army to sail with you. I am sure the griffins are not your only concern. Those that man the ship cannot always be trusted."

"Send word as soon as we are ready to sail."

Reginald nodded and drew a fist to his chest. As Gautier turned to leave, he was surprised to see Velsa standing in the open doorway. Taking a deep breath, he walked toward her and saw her smile slowly fade. He was sure she had heard he would be leaving the island.

"Gautier, I didn't know that you had returned until I passed Lord Heinrich in the hallway. He tells me you are leaving again," she said, as she lifted her hand attempting to stroke his face.

Stepping back to avoid her touch, he saw her confused expression.

"Velsa, don't look so confused. I have told you before, that I will not tolerate these acts of affection in front of the army. I don't tolerate it from them; therefore, I should follow my own rules."

"Gautier, I am sorry. I couldn't help myself. You have been gone such a long time. I have missed you."

"I was on my way to see you, but since you already know I am leaving, I need to prepare for my journey to Crownnail."

Velsa stepped back to allow Gautier to leave and watched him until the hallway turned, and he was gone from view. She sensed something had changed between them. His words had been cold and uncaring. When he spoke, his eyes had never found hers. With a heavy sigh, she resolved in her mind that it had to be the sudden voyage to retrieve the Lady Petula that had him upset. After all, she had done nothing to cause his withdrawal from her. She would wait until he returned. By then, he would miss her, and she would be secure in his arms again.

* * *

It had been three days of feeling trapped like a prisoner in her cottage before Kayleigh finally decided to wander beyond her porch. Even the morning sunrise she loved had not been enough to lure her to step outside. She had filled her days with making jelly from the berries she had collected and scrubbing the mud from her floor. After using her last candle the night before, she was faced with sitting in the dim light of the fire in her hearth once darkness claimed the sky.

Upset that she had let Gautier intimidate her, she tugged on her boots and tightened the laces. Stomping her feet in frustration, she was determined to put an end to it. Snatching her basket and shawl, she opened her door and inhaled the salty air. More than prepared for a chance meeting, she slammed the door behind her.

Suddenly remembering the wild onions she had promised to bring to Big John, she prayed the storm had not ruined them. Deciding to take a shortcut instead of the usual worn path, she made her way over the moss covered rocks and tiptoed through a small stream that had been created from the recent storm. Reaching the spot where the thin stalks had once stood so proudly, she was dismayed to find that they had been beaten down by the heavy rain. Tugging on a few battered stalks, she was relieved to see the small white bulbs had been protected beneath the ground. Pulling all that remained and putting them in her basket, she made her way towards Big John's Market to fulfill her promise.

It wasn't long before she reached the village square and found it was crowded with people selling their wares. Kayleigh cautiously looked about for any sign of Gautier. Noticing several horses tethered in front of the tavern, she searched for the boar and thistle markings. Seeing none, she walked past the small open stable and peered inside to find it empty. With a sigh of relief, she felt her body relax. He was gone. Thankful for his absence, she could now return to her simple life and keep her secret hidden.

* * *

Wagons lined the harbor at Cobb Cove. They were each waiting to be unloaded onto the ship Lucinda May for the voyage to Crownnail Island. Gautier and Reginald had walked the ship from bow to stern inspecting everything to insure the ship's worthiness. Pleased with what they had seen, Reginald ordered the cargo to be brought aboard and stowed.

Great care had been given to the small cabin that would serve as Lady Petula's quarters. Three slim beds had been built into the cabin walls. Each were covered with a thick mattress stuffed with feathers and dressed with linen coverlets. A table that had been secured to the floor was surrounded by four small chairs. Lanterns filled with thick candles hung from the heavy beamed ceiling. They may have seemed extreme to those that slept in hammocks strung from the ceiling, but Lord Heinrich demanded that she be given as much comfort as possible. This was her first voyage, and Gautier wanted it to be comfortable for his brother's sake.

After watching the barrels of fresh water, ale, root vegetables, apples, and dried meat loaded onto the ship, Gautier followed three men carrying locked chests into the cabin he had chosen for himself. The first chest contained gold coins for Lord Larchmont. It was a gift from his brother in appreciation for the approval of Petula's hand. The second chest of gold would secure food and water for the return trip to Alltree. The last chest was filled with gold and silver trinkets, crystals, and gemstones for the griffins. If needed, it would be an offering in return for safe passage. The griffins were known to be fierce in battle and faithful guardians of Crownnail Island. Once mated, they became ferocious killers if any sign of aggression was displayed toward their mates or the island. Gautier hoped it would be enough to ward off the beasts.

After leaving his cabin, he noticed Reginald standing at the gangplank. Next to him were three members of his army. He recognized all of them and knew them to be trustworthy.

"My Lord, everything has been loaded, and the captain is waiting for your command," said Reginald. "Carney, Lorcan, and Hugh will be making the voyage with you. Do you have any words for them before I take to dry land?"

Gautier nodded and gripped Carney's shoulder.

"It is good to have you aboard, and I hope this will be a smooth voyage for us all. I am trusting the captain and his crew to see us safely to and from our destination, but be mindful of the cargo we carry. It would be reason enough to end us in return for the prize."

The men responded with their fists against their chests and then stepped back allowing their commander to disembark. Stepping onto the gangplank, Reginald turned and looked back at Gautier.

"Have you noticed Velsa? She has been standing on the dock hoping to speak with you before you sail. I wouldn't allow her to come aboard, and she threatened to turn me into a snake."

Gautier smirked and stepped forward to have a clear view of the dock. Seeing her lift her hand to wave at him, he stepped back to speak to Reginald.

"I hadn't been looking for her, but to save you the suffering, I will speak with her."

Making their way down to the bottom of the gangplank, Gautier reached for his commander's arm. Pulling him close, he gripped his shoulders before he leaned in to speak to him.

"I leave Black Thistle in your care. Keep it safe and watch after my brother for me."

"My Lord, you honor me with your trust. I will keep all you care for safe. Now, say your good-byes and set sail for Crownnail."

Gautier released his commander and watched him boldly walk past Velsa. The two of them had never been friends. Reginald had tolerated her to please him, and she had looked for ways to divide them without success.

"Gautier, I have come to wish you a safe voyage and tell you that I will miss you."

"There was no need to come all this way. I have little time before we sail. The captain is waiting."

She tried to wrap her arms around his waist, but he grabbed her arms and gently pushed her back.

"Velsa, look at me. You will soil your gown."

"I will get a new one if it is soiled. I want to hold you in my arms before you leave."

She broke free of his hold and wrapped her arms around his waist. Feeling nothing, he rested his hands upon her shoulders until she pulled back. The hurt look upon her face was obvious, but there was nothing he could do to change the way he felt. It was over between them. Someone else held his heart. If he could figure out a delicate way to remove her from his life, they would all benefit.

"Now, be off with you. This is no place for a lady. I have a mission to complete. The sooner I leave; the sooner I will return."

Eager to leave her, he turned and climbed the gangplank as quickly as he could. Fearing she would follow him, he turned and waved good-bye.

Velsa stood waving her hand and watching the ship cut through the water as it made its way out of Cobb Cove. Seeing him wave back at her, she realized she had nothing to worry about, or did she?

Chapter 3

It was early evening, and the sun was starting to sink into the sea. The sky was a colorful delight full of beautiful shades of blue, pink, and orange. As Gautier stood on the bow of the ship, he could see an ominous dark cloud off in the distance. They had been lucky to sail through four days of good weather, and the threat of a storm coming at night was more than worrisome.

Seeing the captain out of the corner of his eye, he pointed toward the darkness.

"Do you see it? A storm is coming," cautioned Gautier.

"I have been watching the storm cloud and notified the crew to prepare for rough seas," the captain replied, as he took his place beside Gautier.

"It seems to be moving very quickly, in our direction, and I find it strange that there is only one dark cloud."

"One dark cloud often leads the storm, but other more dangerous clouds may follow close behind, My Lord. We'll do our best to avoid them. Lucinda May has been through many a storm, and she'll not give into this one."

"Captain, I hope that to be true."

Gautier left the captain in search of Carney. He found him helping the crew tightening the lashings to secure everything on the deck.

"My Lord, take your meal," shouted Carney. "The fires in the galley will be smothered soon. The captain fears a cooking fire could be flung about the galley during the storm. We won't have another meal until it has passed."

"Where are Lorcan and Hugh?"

"Helping the crew below deck to secure the cannons and batten down the hatches."

As Gautier turned to go in search of Lorcan and Hugh, he could hear the captain ordering the striking of the royals, and he looked up to see the crew handling the small sails at the top of the mast. The lower sails were filling with air making them bulge from the pressure of the wind, and small funnels of wind were beginning to swirl about the deck. A sudden gust of wind pushed against his back throwing him toward the open doorway to the lower deck. Gripping the threshold to keep from falling, Gautier swore to himself, "Lucinda May, I'll lend you all the magic I possess. In return, I ask that you keep your part of the bargain and get us to Crownnail in one piece."

* * *

Cadfan stood at the edge of the stone ledge looking down at Featherstone Castle. He could see the guards were busy bringing the evening's lanterns to flame, and candlelight was beginning to flicker against the stained glass windows. He felt his shoulders relax as he took in the fiery orange orb low in the sky. The view of the castle against the warm colors of the sunset had always been his favorite, and it beckoned him to take to the sky.

Closing his eyes, he gave himself over to the spirit within him and let the griffin come forth. Hearing the scrapping of his talons against the stone, he ruffled is feathers and lifted his wings preparing to take flight. He knew himself to be handsome and took pride in his majestic appearance. It was the amber feathers on the back of his wings that set him apart from the rest of the griffins on Crownnail and what attracted the females.

"Cadfan," shouted Henwas. "Why aren't you gone? Be off with you. The commander says the ship carrying the Black

Thistle Guard should be nearing the island, and they will need safe passage. All of the rumors we heard of rogue griffins are no longer rumors. The only survivor from the Red Ruby Anne was able to describe their attackers. From his description, we believe it to be Efron and his band of followers. Banishing them from the island did little to protect the sea."

Bowing his head in acknowledgement, Cadfan turned and leapt up into the sky. The sound of his wings beating against the night air was all that Henwas could hear as he stood and watched the griffin head out to sea.

Cadfan could see a tall ship off in the distance. Its flag whipped in the wind; however, the markings of the boar and thistle were clearly visible. He knew this to be the ship that would escort Lady Petula back to Alltree Island to meet Lord Heinrich, her future husband. On Krega's orders, he had been sent to see that the ship and its passengers arrived safely. The sea was full of pirates willing to strip a ship of its glory, leaving the ship ablaze and its crew left floating in the sea if they were lucky.

It was obvious that the ship and the storm were heading directly for each other. It wouldn't be long before the storm would be directly over them, and they would be at its mercy. Cadfan feared the protection he could offer would do little to help the vessel. He would have to rely on the skill of the captain and crew to see them through. If the storm left nothing of the ship but scattered debris, his only protection would be to pluck them from the sea.

Unable to maintain his position with the wind swirling about him, Cadfan flew toward the ship and calmer air. The ship's only chance of avoiding the storm was to sail to clear skies. Looking about, he noticed a narrow path that might offer them an escape. Racing toward the ship, he drew the attention of the nervous crew. Slowing his approach upon seeing their raised arms holding weapons, he noticed someone of prominence waving his arms and shouting. Seeing them lower their weapons, Cadfan flew down toward the men.

"Follow me. You must follow me," Cadfan shouted. "Look off the port side. The path to safety is narrow, but if you hurry, your chance of avoiding the wrath of this storm will be much higher."

"Captain, you heard the griffin! Follow him," Gautier shouted.

The captain shook his head in confusion but shouted the order. The men scrambled to obey, more from fear of the creature than the storm.

Gautier nodded his head in thanks at the griffin and shouted, "Lead the way, my friend."

Cadfan flew up over the top of the mast and headed in the direction he hoped would take them to safety.

The captain and crew were doing their best to follow the griffin. Now that the ship had turned and was sailing across the wind, they could feel the waves crashing against the side of the ship. As the storm drew nearer, the darkened sky made it almost impossible to see the griffin. The captain could only see a vague silhouette of his wings off in the distance. While the captain kept his eye on the griffin, Gautier stood on the starboard side of the ship with his arms raised pushing his magic at the storm trying to keep it at bay. He had forced the wind back, but the rain had taken its place, and it pelted him and everyone else on deck.

As the waves crashed against the side of the ship, the sea water made its way over the railings and onto the deck. With the deck's planks covered with water, Gautier knew that the seams of rope and tar would eventually wash away allowing the water to seep below deck. It wasn't long before the captain sent a few of the crew below to man the pumps. With the ship's belly full of rocks to provide stability, the ship would surely sink fast if too much water was allowed to settle at the bottom.

Fear was seen in more than one man's eyes as the crew struggled to tether themselves to prevent being washed overboard. The sound of the waves was deafening as one after another slammed against the side of the ship. Gautier could hear the strain of the mast against the wind. He knew if the mast snapped they could all be killed. With one hand aimed at the mast and one at the storm clouds, he felt the last of his magic drain from his body as he collapsed to the deck.

* * *

The storm had passed and the early morning light cast a soft pink glow about the sky. The Lucinda May sat drifting in calm water with torn sails hanging from her yards. Gautier tried to open his eyes, but the salt water stung and made it difficult to see. The only sounds he could hear were the lapping of gentle waves against the ship and the slapping of the wet sails above him. If it hadn't been for the griffin, he was sure they would have all perished in the storm. Lifting his head from the rough surface of the deck, he took stock of his surroundings.

Men were sprawled about the deck with ropes still tied around their waists. Searching for Carney, he forced himself up on all fours. His arms were aching, and his mind was hazy. Feeling someone take his arm, he looked up to see Lorcan.

"My Lord, let me help you," he said, as he held Gautier's arm and helped him to stand.

"Where is Hugh and Carney?" asked Gautier.

"Hugh is below. He took a nasty blow to the head, but he will survive. I haven't seen Carney. He wasn't below, so he must be somewhere up here."

The men turned to see the captain untying his tether and heading for a man slumped over a crate. One by one, the men woke and gathered on the deck waiting for orders from their captain. Carney wasn't among them and feared to be lost at sea.

"I need some help," one of the crew shouted.

He was tugging on a rope that hung over the port side of the ship. A few men came to his aid and heaved on the thick length of the rope. At its end was a body that had been battered by the waves against the side of the ship. It was Carney. The men carefully laid him on the deck and untied the rope about his waist. As they stepped back, Gautier and Lorcan stepped forward.

"Captain . . . Carney has had enough of the sea. Put him in my cabin. He needs a peaceful sleep during the rest of our voyage. We will take his body to Crownnail," declared Gautier. "Once there, I will build the pyre myself."

"Take him below. Do your best to clean and bind his body," ordered the captain. "When you're done, we have sails to mend."

"Lorcan, go with the men to see after Carney," choked Gautier. "I will see to the sails."

Three of the crew helped Lorcan lift Carney's limp battered body, and Gautier watched as they made their way below deck.

Furious that he had lost Carney, Gautier raised his arms with clenched fists. They were shaking, and he could feel his nails biting into the flesh of his palms. After growling a few phrases, he opened his fists to allow bright light to fly through the air towards the torn sails. The light swirled around the yards as they reattached the sails and mended the canvas. A few of the crew stood bewildered at the display of his magic, and others squatted while covering their heads, afraid they would be harmed by the bright lights. After seeing they were all repaired, he turned to find Hugh, but the sound of beating wings could be heard above him. Looking up, he saw the griffin hovering near the ship.

"Did you suffer much?" asked Cadfan.

"Greatly," replied Gautier. "Had it not been for your help, the cold dark water of the sea would have taken us all."

"I am sorry I could not do more," he apologized.

"You did your best. Now, lead us safely to Crownnail," ordered Gautier.

The griffin bowed his head and lifted up into the sky.

"Follow the griffin," shouted the captain.

Gautier turned and headed toward the lower deck to see after his men.

* * *

With the island in sight, what appeared to be a stone castle built high into the side of the mountain was the first thing Gautier noticed as he stood at the bow of the ship. Due to its unusual location, he determined it must have been built to prevent an attack from the enemy. Why else would a castle have no visible path leading to its entrance.

As they entered the harbor of the crescent shaped island, the griffin landed on the dock and immediately shifted into his human form. He was greeted by several men that stood waiting to help with the lines in securing the ship. Two other men sat upon a wagon, and a single rider held the reins of five horses.

"Send word to Lord Larchmont that Lord Gautier has arrived." Cadfan ordered the young man on horseback as he took the reins of the horses. "I will escort them to Featherstone shortly."

With reins in hand, Cadfan watched as the gangplank was lowered, and Lord Gautier made his way down the wooden plank toward him.

"My Lord, I welcome you to Crownnail Island. My name is Cadfan.," he said, as he bowed his head.

"Cadfan, it is good to finally be on dry land. Again, I thank you," Gautier replied, as he gripped his outstretched hand.

"Krega, my commander, sends his apologies for not being here to greet you. He is at Aderyn's bedside. They are awaiting the birth of their child."

"By her side is where he should be at a moment like this. There are no apologies needed."

Gautier glanced again at the castle set into the stones of the mountain and over at the wagon. Cadfan could see the sadness upon his face.

"I am truly sorry for your loss. The men will see to removing your man's body from the ship, and the wagon is prepared to carry him to the castle. If you have anything else you wish to have unloaded, the wagon will return for it."

"There are several chests in my cabin. Lorcan will stay behind to see after them until your wagon returns, and there is no need to bring him a horse. He can ride on the wagon."

Gautier heard the captain shout and turned to see the crew standing in two lines as Lorcan, Hugh, and two other men carried Carney's body between them. As they made their way down the gangplank, those that stood about the dock bowed their bared heads as Carney's body was loaded onto the wagon.

"How will the wagon maneuver the steep path?" Gautier asked, as he looked up at the mountain and then back at Cadfan.

"My Lord, that isn't Featherstone Castle. It is the griffin's sanctuary." He lifted his arm and pointed to the stone towers that stood above the top of the trees. "That is Featherstone."

Gautier looked beyond the shelter of the trees at three grey stone towers that held flags of deep sapphire bearing a plume of five golden feathers. He had not seen the castle as they approached the island and didn't notice it as they entered the harbor.

"Featherstone is well hidden from the sea. All that was visible was your sanctuary upon the mountain."

"It is the Eyes of Crownnail. Our sanctuary has deterred many a ship that thought to take this island for their own. If they were brave enough to venture to its shore, the griffins taking flight from its stone ledges were enough to change their mind. We have protected Crownnail for a very long time, and will do so as long as it is required."

Gautier raised his eyebrows as he imagined several griffins flying toward an unsuspecting ship prepared to shred the sails from their masts. The sight would have shaken him in his boots.

Seeing Hugh had taken his place upon the wagon beside Carney's body, he called to Lorcan, "Stay behind with the chests. The wagon will return for them."

Lorcan nodded and quickly made his way back aboard the ship.

"Shall we go?" asked Cadfan, as he handed Gautier the reins to his horse and then tied the other three horses to the back of the wagon.

Gautier mounted the horse he was offered and waited for Cadfan to take the lead. As he followed behind him, he thought of how long he had known his friend. As young boys, he had taught Carney to swim and throw a dagger. He had spent many nights with him in the tavern drinking ale and watching him flirt with the ladies. Since he had no mate or family to mourn him, he knew it was up to him to keep his memory alive.

The gate to Featherstone Castle was open wide, and the castle guards lined the entrance. Just ahead, standing before a set of carved wooden doors stood Lord Peter and Lady Tula. Next to her father, Lady Petula stood holding her father's hand. She was a wisp of a young woman. Her hair was as black as a raven's wing, and her skin was pale with a hint of rose upon her cheeks.

Bringing his horse to a stop, Gautier dismounted and approached Lord Larchmont. With a quick bow of his head, he waited to be addressed.

"Lord Gautier, we welcome you to Featherstone," Peter greeted Gautier with a firm handshake.

Tula stepped forward and offered her hand to Gautier.

"Lady Larchmont," Gautier said, as he kissed the back of her hand.

"We were sorry to hear of your troublesome voyage and are saddened by your loss."

"Your condolences are appreciated, My Lady."

"I have given orders to make preparations for the pyre. I hope you will find them acceptable," Peter said, as he firmly grasped Gautier's shoulder.

"You have honored me with your hospitality, My Lord."

"Petula, come meet Lord Gautier," requested her father.

Petula stepped forward and made a deep curtsy. She raised her eyes to Gautier and gave him a timid smile.

"Lord Gautier, it is an honor to meet you," she shyly offered.

"Lady Petula, the honor is mine."

"Let's get all of you settled. Cadfan will show your men to their quarters and make sure your man's body is prepared for his flight to the Otherworld. I have had some refreshments set out for you. Follow me, I will tell you of the plans I have made."

Two guards opened the doors as Lord Peter took Lady Tula's arm to help her up the stone steps. Extending his arm to Lady Petula, Gautier watched as she gracefully took his arm and lifted her skirt to maneuver the steps.

Gautier hadn't noticed the sun had set and left darkness in its place until he saw the guard lighting torches around the hall. The food and wine had been plentiful, and the conversation had been interesting. He found that it was a good distraction from the sadness he felt after losing Carney.

A heavy door groaned and drew everyone's attention. Once fully open, a large man with white hair tied at the nape of his neck entered the hall. There was a wide grin upon his face as he approached Lord Larchmont.

"My Lord, please pardon my intrusion," begged Krega, as he knelt before Lord Peter and bowed his head.

"Do you have good news for us?" asked Peter.

"My Lord, Aderyn has done her work and given me a fine son. He has the lungs of a warrior."

Boisterous cheers and clapping filled the hall. As Krega stood, Peter grabbed his hand and shoulder to offer him his congratulations.

"What name has he been given?" asked Peter.

"We shall call him Brice. It was Aderyn's desire to name our son Brice."

"It is a good strong name."

"How is Aderyn?" asked Tula.

"Tired and happy to be done with it, My Lady. I left her sleeping with the babe at her breast."

"Please give her my congratulations. I will visit her and the child when she is ready to receive me."

"As you wish, My Lady. I will not intrude upon you and yours any longer. My place is by Aderyn's side."

Krega bowed his head, turned, and left through the open doorway.

As the laughter and excitement of Krega's news quieted, Lord Peter drew everyone's attention.

"Tonight we will send Carney, a member of the Evergreen Army, to the Otherworld. Please follow me."

Gautier followed Lord Peter, Lady Tula, and Lady Petula through the castle hallways and out into the night air. There, they walked along a crushed stone path that took them to a large pond almost entirely surrounded by trees. Several torches had been brought to flame around the water's edge, and their amber light reflected in the still water. An archer stood at attention across the pond from where Gautier had been led. In the center of the pond, he could see a wooden raft holding Carney's body covered in a blanket of sheer gold silk. Resting against his body was his polished sword clasped in his once powerful hands.

"Shall I speak or do you wish to address my people?" asked Peter.

Stepping forward to face the small gathering, Gautier looked at all of the somber faces.

"We sailed toward Crownnail Island to retrieve a young woman, your Lady Petula, to become my brother's bride. It was a voyage of good things to come for the people of Black Thistle Castle. On the way, the darkness of a storm at sea took the life of Carney McFarland. He was brave, sometimes stubborn, funny, and faithful to me, my brother, and Black Thistle Castle. It is my honor to send him from this world to the Otherworld."

Gautier turned to face the pond. As he did, the archer placed his arrow into the flame of the torch that stood beside him. Gautier watched as he aimed the arrow toward the sky and then released it. The burning tip of the arrow flew up into the air and then fell down upon Carney's silk draped body. Instantly the wooden raft was engulfed in flames. Over his shoulder, Gautier could hear everyone kneeling. Pursing his lips to keep from crying out, he felt Petula take his hand in her own.

"Do not be sad, my brother. Those that have gone before him will greet him with music and singing," she softly whispered.

Chapter 4

The sun had barely risen when Gautier arrived at the dock the next morning. He had passed one empty wagon on its way back to Featherstone and knew that two loaded wagons were following close behind him. It would be a busy morning loading the supplies he had procured from Lord Peter's stocks and the people of a nearby village. They had been more than generous and given him the best of what they had to offer. In return, he had made sure they were paid well for their kindness.

Hearing a familiar sound, he looked up to see a griffin with white feathers covering the underside of its black wings and gold bands about his front legs. As it landed, it instantly shifted into human form.

"Lord Gautier, does this day find you rested?" asked Krega, as he stood with his arms crossed over his chest displaying the gold bands upon his wrists.

"Rested but eager to return to Black Thistle," he replied.

Seeing Krega's furrowed brow, he feared he had offended him and made an effort to apologize.

"My time here was meant to be short. I had not planned on the storm or its brutal outcome. Had it not been for Cadfan's help, we would have all perished."

"He is one of our best."

Hearing the rumbling of wooden wheels, both men stepped back as a horse drawn wagon full of fine chests displaying the golden plume of five feathers came to a stop. Men jumped from the wagon and started unloading it.

"I have come here this morning to offer you an escort through the waters that surround Crownnail and beyond if needed. Cadfan and Henwas have been chosen to protect you and the Lady Petula."

"It is clear we are no match for the bitter storms that plague the sea. Your offer is graciously accepted."

"Good, it is not only the storms that plague the sea that cause the need for the benefit of an escort. Many pirates sail the sea. Human and griffin pirates take what they can from those that cannot defend themselves. They are fearless and deadly. Since you will fly a Featherstone flag beneath Black Thistle's on your return voyage, they will know the cargo is precious and be more than tempted to attack."

"For some reason, I fear the storms more than the pirates."

"Hopefully, you will not find either. Tell the captain to sound the bell once you are ready to depart. Cadfan and Henwas will hear it and take to the skies. They will escort you beyond Mermaid Fin Rock. From there, you should be free of any danger."

"I will, and thank you."

Gautier offered his hand to Krega, but he did not return the gesture. Feeling a bit uncomfortable, he withdrew his hand and searched his mind for something to say.

"Krega, I wish you great joy with your son, Brice."

Krega bowed his head in thanks and made his way to the path that led back to Featherstone. There, he shifted back into his griffin form and flew toward the sanctuary.

Gautier's puzzled stare at the magnificent griffin was interrupted by the sound of more wagons. Looking up, he saw Hugh jumping from the back of one of the wagons stacked with crates filled with chickens. His forehead was bound, and feathers littered his tunic and hair.

"Sleeping with the chickens, I see," laughed Gautier.

"My Lord, I am sorry to say that they were the only ladies that took a liking to me," replied Hugh, as he brushed the feathers from his hair and shoulders. "I will be glad to return to Black Thistle where my talents are truly appreciated."

"I see the blow to your head has not hampered your bragging. Best you get onboard the ship and see that the supplies are loaded properly."

Hugh nodded and stepped around to the side of the wagon to speak to the driver, "Grab a crate or two, and I will show you where to stow the plump little ladies."

Seeing the broad grin upon Hugh's face helped overshadow some of the sadness he felt over the loss of Carney.

* * *

Lady Petula stood holding her father's hand as the last of the chests were loaded onto the Lucinda May. As Gautier approached Lord Peter, he noticed the tears that fell upon Lady Tula's cheeks.

"Lord Peter, I will see that your daughter is safely brought to Black Thistle Castle. Lord Heinrich has given his word that Lady Petula will be allowed the freedom to make her own decision regarding the marriage. He desires it to be a good match bound by love. If she finds she carries love in her heart for Lord Heinrich, you will be invited to a grand wedding. If her heart feels nothing, she need only ask for passage back to you."

Lady Petula wrapped her arms around her father's waist and pressed her face against his chest. He kissed the top of her head and quietly whispered for her to kiss her mother good-bye. Gautier looked down at his boots to give them one last moment of privacy together.

"Lord Gautier, I put my most precious gift in your hands," Peter said, as he lifted his daughter's hand and placed it upon Gautier's open palm. "Guard her with your life."

Taking hold of her small hand, he smiled to reassure her. With his other hand fisted over his heart, he looked at Lord Peter.

"I promise you, Lord Peter. I will guard her as if she were my own daughter. I will willingly give my life to protect her."

Peter nodded and stepped back from his daughter as he clutched Tula's trembling hand. He feared if he stood too close, he would grab his daughter and run with her back to Featherstone Castle.

Gautier guided Lady Petula up the gangplank followed by her two handmaids, Ella and Annalee. Both were fair in face with hair the color of honey. The twin sisters had been with Petula since her eleventh birthday. They were more like sisters to Petula than handmaids, and they had lovingly taken care of her. With Gautier behind them, Petula and the girls stood at the rail waving to her parents one last time.

"My Lord, everything has been stowed and the captain is ready to sail," announced Lorcan.

"Tell the captain to ring the ship's bell. Krega has given us an escort for protection."

He heard the girls gasp and knew that they were afraid. It would be up to him to calm their fears. The bell began to ring, and Gautier looked up at the sanctuary to find two griffins had taken to the skies. He raised his hand to bid Crownnail farewell and hoped for a safe voyage.

"My Lady, when you are ready, I will escort you to your cabin. It is small, but I believe that you will find it comfortable. Your handmaids will share your cabin. I thought you would enjoy their company."

She did not turn around to face him, but he saw her nod as she raised her hand to wipe a tear from her cheek before she spoke, "Is he kind, my Gerwig? Is he a kind man?"

"He is kind, My Lady. You mustn't worry."

She waved one last time to her parents and turned to face him.

"I am ready to retire to my cabin, My Lord."

"It would please me if you called me Gautier. I may be your brother soon and you my little sister."

She could see a pleasant smile upon his face.

"Only if you call me Petula."

Gautier bowed and offered his arm to her, "Let's get you settled, Petula."

* * *

They had been blessed with clear skies and calm water for two days. Unfortunately, the occasional gentle breeze had barely been enough to fill Lucinda May's sails. This was adding too much time to the voyage, and Gautier longed to be home. More than that, he longed to see Madame White and her white wolf again.

Cadfan and Henwas had patrolled the skies; however, there had been nothing more than a few sea birds attracted to the scrapes that had been tossed overboard to claim their attention. After most of each day in the air, they needed to rest. Henwas had taken to perching upon the bow of the ship. Beneath his talons, the elaborately hand-carved Lady Lucinda May guided the way as she sat leaning forward holding a lantern in her outstretched arm. With her other hand, she held the bodice of her gown against the bottom of her corset while exposing her bare breasts to the cool spray of the sea to cool her from the heat of the sun. Cadfan eased his wings by clinging to the crow's nest. He found it to be a bit strange since he had never seen a crow on the open sea.

Petula and her maids left their cabin to walk about the deck twice a day. Once when the sun was high in the sky and then again as the sun was setting. After the first day at sea, she no longer looked back towards Crownnail with tears in her eyes. She had taken to standing at the bow of the ship to welcome her future. Seeing her standing with her hands resting upon the railings, Gautier approached Petula and quietly took his place beside her.

"Do you have someone waiting for you at Black Thistle Castle?" Petula asked.

"There are many that wait for me," he replied.

"Have you a mate?"

"I have no mate."

"Do you desire one?"

"I hope to have a mate one day."

Petula stared at the water. It was as if she could see something that no one else could see.

"Tell me about Black Thistle Castle. I would like to know something of this place that will soon be my new home. The name brings forth a bit of fear within me."

"I hope my description of my home will dispel your fears. It is really quite beautiful."

As she looked up at him, he smiled but saw the concern in her eyes.

"The name comes from the black stones that were used to build the castle. Large stones were cut from the walls of Wispet Canyon and painstakingly hauled up its side to fashion the castle. Large patches of bright purple thistles surrounded the area where the castle was to be built, and my mother refused to allow them to be removed. Oddly enough, it was my mother that offered the name. My father thought it to be fearsome sounding and would be sure to keep danger away. My mother thought it to be beautiful, and she frequently filled her bedchamber with the unusual flowers. It pleased them both in their own way. When you see it, you can decide if it is beautiful or you fear the sight of it."

"I believe that you have lessened my fears."

"Petula, it is not so different from Featherstone. You will find dim hallways, stone floors, towers, and the sounds of flags that whip in the wind. I only ask that you try to see the light that I see when I walk its hallways. There are fires in the hearths that warm us, smiles upon the faces that greet us each day, and the sound of laughter to fill our souls. You need only look beyond your fear to see it. When you do, it will lighten your heart as it has mine."

"You have given me a vision of warm purple light that surrounds my new home. I find I am eager to see it."

"Little sister . . . you are not the only one that is eager to see it." He looked down at her sweet face and saw the first glimpse of a smile that had not shielded tears that were ready to fall. Pleased he had soothed her fears, he patted her hand. "For now, I will leave you to the coming sunset." Gautier stepped back and bowed. "Ladies, I wish you a good evening."

Turning to leave, he heard the screech from Cadfan flying overhead and saw him descending. As he started to land on the quarterdeck, he quickly shifted into his human form.

"My Lord, I have need of you. Please, a word," he shouted.

From the tone of his voice, Gautier felt a troubling sense of doom press down upon his chest as he made his way up the steps.

"There is a ship heading in our direction. It will be here by morning," explained Cadfan. "I caught a faint shadow of it on the horizon."

"I assume it is a pirate ship from the sound of your voice." Gautier replied, as he lowered his voice trying to keep his conversation private.

"Henwas and I will fly as close as we dare and report back to you. Until we return, stay vigilant. I suggest you move the ladies to their cabin."

"Call Henwas to join you for an evening patrol. I don't want to alarm the ladies needlessly."

"Don't wait too long to see them below. Darkness easily hides the enemy, and you must listen for the sound of beating wings."

"How will I know you from the enemy?"

"My griffin will call to you with three short bursts and one long to follow. This way you will know it is safe."

"We will be waiting. Now, go find out what trouble comes our way."

Cadfan nodded and lifted up into the air while changing into his griffin as he called to Henwas. Feeling the urgency of his call, he too took flight and followed after him.

* * *

The sky was dark and Cadfan knew that it would offer them some protection during their flight; however, if the pirates were griffins, they would be alerted to the sound of their beating wings. Separating in the air to approach the ship from both sides, Cadfan and Henwas searched the anchored ship for anything that would confirm his suspicions. A few glowing lanterns swayed in the breeze, but the deck was void of men. Swooping down to the ship's bow, Cadfan saw what confirmed his fear. A carved serpent with ruby eyes stared back at him. It was Efron's ship of rogue griffins. As he flew back away from the ship after seeing the serpent, Henwas met him in the air.

"It's the Black Serpent isn't it?" blurted Henwas. "We have to warn Lord Gautier."

"You return to the Lucinda May to protect Lady Petula. I will alert Krega," ordered Cadfan. "We will need the griffin army to protect them. Go now!"

* * *

"Where is Krega?" Cadfan shouted, as he frantically looked about the army's gathering area. "I need Krega, now!"

"He is with Aderyn and his son," Darach replied, as he ran to meet him. "Why aren't you with Lady Petula?"

"I have spotted Efron's ship. I have seen the Black Serpent."

"What's all the shouting?" bellowed Krega, as he approached the men. "Has someone set fire to your feathers?"

"Commander Krega, we have seen the Black Serpent. She was anchored not far from the Lucinda May," replied Cadfan still out of breath. "I noticed a ship as I patrolled the waters.

Henwas and I flew to see if it be a friend or foe. The ship was quiet, but if Efron has scouts, they will surely discover the Featherstone flag in the morning light."

"Darach . . . inform six of our finest men to prepare for a possible fight," ordered Krega. "Lady Petula is in danger, and we have taken a pledge to protect her. It does not matter what danger threatens her, we will give up our lives if needed."

"Will six be enough?" he replied.

"It will have to be enough. It is not wise to leave Featherstone or those we love to defend themselves. Efron is clever, and he would know anchoring his ship near the Lucinda May would draw the griffins from Crownnail."

Darach immediately understood Krega's reasoning. He nodded his agreement and ran to gather the men that would take to the skies.

"I'm sure that Henwas would have warned the captain not to drop anchor. Even though the sails have been less than full for most of the voyage, any distance that can be put between them and the Black Serpent would be helpful," Cadfan said, as he watched Krega pace back and forth before him. Not expecting a response, he tried to think of something that would reassure him. "Are you aware that Lord Gautier wields magic?"

A quick turn of Krega's head and the lifting of one brow was followed by a sly grin.

"I thought I recognized the scent of magic upon him; however, it appeared to be weak. The aura about him was pale and lifeless."

"I saw him fight the storm with his magic. He did all that he could to keep it from tearing the ship to pieces. When I saw him collapse, I knew that he had nothing left. Had it not been for him, I would have been plucking them from the sea."

"Let's hope that he has rested enough to bring his magic back to full strength. We will need it to fight Efron and his flock of worthless seabirds."

It wasn't long before one griffin after another took to the skies and followed Cadfan and their commander toward the Lucinda May.

* * *

The cover of darkness had shielded the flight of the griffin army from the possibility of being discovered. There were only a few more hours before the sun would rise and Efron's anchor would be hoisted. Finally seeing the ship below them, they flew toward the deck and quickly shifted into their human form as they stepped foot upon the deck. Gautier and the captain stepped forward to meet them.

"This is Commander Krega of Crownnail. You already know Cadfan and Henwas," Gautier introduced the men to the captain.

"Captain," replied Krega with an outstretched hand. "I have brought reinforcements to help protect your ship from the Black Serpent and its foolish feathered pirates." He turned and pointed to his men. This is Darach, Merrick, Haddon, Amren, Cas, Kane, and Badan. They are all good with a blade and bow; however, it will be best if we keep the battle in the air. Our beaks and talons will do much more damage than a single arrow aimed at a griffin's breast."

The captain looked at the men before him with some apprehension, and Krega offered a broad grin in return.

"Don't let the tales told to curious children about our kind fool you," he cautioned. "Griffins are strong and fierce in battle. We have done much more than protect the treasure of shiny objects for Lord Peter. We have protected Crownnail Island from any enemy that has threatened her, and we will do our best to protect you."

"Forgive me if I seem unsure of all that I have seen," replied the captain. "These visions are strange to me. I have seen light shooting from a man's hands and flying eagles with the tail of a lion." The captain stood shaking his head. "This is what a man sees after too much ale or during the fit of a raging fever."

The men began to laugh, and Krega gave them a threatening glare. A sudden quiet surrounded the commander as he looked back at the captain.

"The sun will be upon us soon, and the enemy will surely find us. Let's prepare for what is to come. Men, find a good position to defend this vessel. Under no circumstances are you to allow harm to come to Lady Petula. Kane, I put you in charge of guarding her cabin door. If the ship is breached, you must slip away and take her back to Featherstone."

Kane nodded and took off in search of her cabin.

"Cas, take down the Featherstone flag. Efron knows the plume of five feathers and will know the ship's cargo if he sees it," ordered Krega. "Lord Gautier, I hear that you wield magic, and I need to know of your talents. Magic could be very useful during the fight. Come, walk with me."

The captain pulled his cap from his head and ran his hand over the bald spot it had covered. He watched Krega and Gautier walk toward the bow of the ship while Krega's men scattered. Grasping the medal he wore around his neck, he looked up at the stars.

"I know I must be crazy," he mumbled. "Who would believe what I have seen? If I ever tell this tale, they will surely lock me up. One way or another, I will not speak of it. I'll either keep secret what I have seen or be silenced by my death. Either way, no one will hear of it."

Trying to swallow, he could feel the dryness in his throat and yearned for an ale to ready the problem. He pulled his cap back on his head and headed for his cabin in search of a much needed cup of ale.

***

Gautier looked up when he heard the sudden snap of the sails filling with air. He could feel the ship begin to cut through the water and felt some relief in the swaying motion. While searching the horizon for any sight of the Black Serpent, he found nothing but the gradual lightning of the sky. Pleased with its absence, he slapped the railing and turned to find Krega walking toward him.

"If Efron's scouts have seen this ship, they will catch us. You can be sure of it," smirked Krega. "We won't be able to outrun the speed of the Black Serpent."

"They are nowhere in sight. How could they possibly catch us?" Gautier asked.

"The Black Serpent is much larger with many more sails. She will fly through the water once her sails catch the wind."

"You sound as if all is lost. Why not take Lady Petula and return to Featherstone? My brother would not want her put in danger."

"Sailing the open sea has already put her in danger. There are many more pirates ready to pillage merchant vessels than Efron's flock of rogue seabirds. Your wise captain has been cautious and taken the safest routes."

"He has been lucky is what you mean to say?"

"Yes, your captain has been very lucky."

Gautier ran his hands over his face trying to think. His magic would provide some protection, but once his magic was spent, he would be worthless.

"How much time before they catch us?"

"When the sun is at its highest, we will see the flag bearing the Black Serpent. Until then, we prepare and wait."

"Shouldn't you be in the sky? You could see them coming. You could give us ample warning."

"If they haven't seen Cadfan and Henwas, they won't know that we are on the ship. Surprise will give us an advantage. If they know that we are here, we will see the griffins long before we see the Black Serpent."

"Then, let's hope for clear skies."

Krega nodded and slapped Gautier on the shoulder.

"Well, let's take our morning meal," said Gautier. "The captain will order the fires be put out, and I would prefer cooked eggs to slurping them raw from their shells."

Gautier suddenly thought he may have offended Krega and started to apologize. He was cut short before he could finish with the sound of Krega's laughter.

"I stand before you as a man with a growling belly of a lion. Whatever is put upon my plate will do fine."

* * *

The captain's crew and Krega's men had kept constant watch all morning for the Black Serpent. Just as Krega had said, it had pierced the blue horizon when the sun was near its highest point in the sky. It seemed like it was racing toward them, and Gautier watched as the dark smudge grew larger and larger. Even though the Lucinda May was barreling through the water, it wasn't long before they could all see the serpent upon the flag as it whipped in the strong breeze.

After hearing the warning bell, Lady Petula took her last breath of fresh air and hurried to her cabin. Fearing what might happen, she and her handmaids nervously huddled on her bed within their cabin. She knew of Efron's hatred for her father and had seen his wickedness firsthand. He had torn the feathered wings from a young griffin because her father had denied him her hand. As a result, her father had acted quickly and banished Efron from the island. Now that she was beyond her father's protection, she feared what he might do to her.

"My Lady, do not make a sound. No matter what you hear, do not make a sound or draw attention to yourselves. Keep your door locked," ordered Kane. "If I shout Brimstone, you must quickly open the door to allow me to carry you safely away. If I shout Violet, the danger will have passed and you are safe. No other words should draw you to the door. Do you understand?"

"Yes, I understand," called Petula, as the women huddled closer together.

Krega's men had tried to disguise themselves the best they could by rubbing tar on their faces and donning woolen caps pulled down against their brows. The few moments they would gain from their disguises could mean the difference between life and death for everyone.

A few men hurried to bring buckets of lime from below deck. A handful of lime thrown at the face of an enemy could render them blind and unable to defend themselves. A blade or dagger to the chest would easily end the advance of their challenge. While fire on deck was a danger, the crew would need it to light the torches dipped in tar that would be thrown onto the enemy's deck.

Gautier stood at the stern of the ship as he listened to the captain shouting orders and kept his eye on the enemy. Off in the distance, he could see dark storm clouds were beginning to form, and it gave the Black Serpent a backdrop of impending doom. The very thought of trying to protect the Lucinda May from pirates, rogue griffins, and another brutal storm was daunting.

Feeling the need to test his magic, he raised his arms and focused on the dark ship that chased them. Before he could release his magic, a thunderous blast and a burst of fire followed by another exploded from the Black Serpent. He could see balls of fire coming toward him and swept his arm to the side causing them to change course. The enemy was aiming for the stern's rudder in hopes of ending the ship's maneuverability in the water, and he knew he had to protect the stern of the ship if they were to survive.

Knowing the captain must have heard the blasts, he waited to see how he would counter the attack. The ship's bow began to move, and it slowly presented its starboard side to the oncoming ship. Gautier ran to the main deck and leaned against the bulwark to steady his body as he raised his arms. Releasing his magic, he tried to slow the oncoming ship, but it was too far away.

Looking up, he saw the gray clouds had covered most of the blue sky. The storm was coming but not fast enough. Clenching his fists, he chanted under his breath, and the clouds grew darker. Rain began to pelt the deck as lightning brightened the sky. With the storm well under way, Gautier refocused his attention on the water that surrounded the Black Serpent. He pushed his magic against the water and caused the waves to smash against her bow until the force was so great she began to turn.

Thinking they had given up their quest, he started to relax until he saw several griffins leap into the air. Not going unnoticed by Krega and his men, he watched as they allowed Efron's griffins to fly away from their ship and the protection it might offer them. At Krega's signal, they leapt into the air, and carefully concealed their griffin bodies behind the sails. Patiently waiting for the right moment, Krega finally gave the command to attack.

Krega and his army raced toward the oncoming enemy. He could see Efron leading the rogue flock, and delighted in the slight moment of hesitation he displayed when he realized who he faced. With talons ready, they eagerly charged forward. Krega met Efron with wings spread and talons bared. As their talons locked, Krega began to kick Efron's body with his hind paws. Efron tried to reach for the place where Krega's wings joined his body, but Krega was quick to impale Efron's neck with his beak. Drawing the first blood heightened his desire to end Efron's life.

As they continued to battle, Amren succumbed to a dislocated wing and pulled back in pain allowing the griffin he fought to race toward the Lucinda May. Cleverly, Krega had left a few of his army behind to defend against such an attack. As the rogue griffin hovered over the bow of the ship, Badan silently glided down and encircled the griffin's neck with his talons. Lifting up into the air, Badan carried him away from the ship. With one swift tear of his beak, the griffin's neck was broken, and he hung lifeless in Badan's talons. He swooped down, and dropped his dead body into the sea. Seeing Amren struggling to return to the ship, Badan flew to help him. With Amren on his back, he carried his wounded body back to the deck of the ship.

Cadfan had dropped his lifeless attacker's body into the sea and watched Henwas do the same. All that remained was the ongoing battle between their commander and Efron. As they neared to offer assistance, Krega pulled back away from them.

"This battle is mine and mine alone. Stand clear and let me finish this," shouted Krega.

Blood dripped from Krega's eye and hind leg. Deep bleeding slashes were splayed across Efron's chest and hind legs. Krega could tell that Efron was weakening and dropped his body beneath his. The weight pulled on Efron, and his wings beat furiously to keep from falling. Krega knew the time was right, Efron was too weak to continue fighting. With all the strength that he had left, he tore Efron's wing from his body. Pain consumed Efron, but he made no sound. Krega looked into his eyes and saw defeat.

"End me now," gasped Efron. "Grant me one final pleasure."

"As you wish," he replied, as he broke his neck with the twist of his beak.

Krega dropped Efron from his talons and watched him fall. As the waves covered him, Krega had already turned toward the Lucinda May. The danger was over, and the Lucinda May was free to return to Alltree Island.

Chapter 5

Velsa sat wringing her hands in her lap. She had been nervous all morning after viewing Gautier's arrival in her crystal sphere. He had acted so strange when he left to retrieve Lady Petula, and she feared he might be tired of her. Tapping her feet nervously against the velvet covered footstool, she considered changing the color of her dress for the third time. She wanted everything to be perfect when he arrived at her chamber door.

Have I assumed too much? What if Gautier doesn't come to see me? What if he doesn't want to see me? I won't take that chance. I'll make sure he sees me. I'll go to him.

Pushing the footstool away with her feet, she stood and brushed the folds from her skirt. For a moment, she twisted the end of her braid between her fingers. Her mind began to wander back to their first meeting, and she quickly pulled the ribbon from the end of her braid. Running her fingers through the woven strands, she let her hair hang loosely around her shoulders. Sure that one look at her would warm his heart, she hurried toward her chamber door. Pulling the door open, she looked down at her skirt. With the nod of her head, her pale green gown turned lavender.

* * *

Lady Petula and her handmaids leaned against the bulwark of the ship and gazed at the stone towers of the castle. Set against a forest of evergreens, she found it was not unlike her own home.

"That is Evergreen Castle," Gautier said, from behind her. "Lord Evergreen was the first to build on Alltree Island. He brought news of the island and others followed his lead, my father included."

"The sunlight reflecting against the castle tower is beautiful. My home was sheltered from the sea by the trees. It did not allow me to see the water from my window. It has been a joy to gaze upon the skies colorful reflection upon the sea," she replied. "Gautier, can you see the sea from Black Thistle Castle?"

"Sadly, you cannot see it; however, there are other wonders that will delight you. The view of Wispet Canyon is breathtaking, and the snow covered Wintergreen Mountains are something to behold. If you travel to Fallon Castle, you will be amazed by the waterfalls that cascade behind the castle."

"I would love to explore them."

"My brother is fascinated by what nature has to offer which means you already have something in common. I am sure he would enjoy exploring them with you."

Petula smiled as she took one last look at Evergreen Castle and then leaned forward to see what was ahead of them. Seeing nothing but cliffs, thatched roofs, and water, she sighed.

"It won't be long before we will enter Cobb Cove, and we can make our way to your new home."

"Is it a long journey?"

"No, we shall be there before the sun begins to set."

Gautier was eager himself to return to the island. Retrieving Lady Petula for his brother had kept him away from Woods Village far too long. As they sailed past a string of small cottages that overlooked the sea, he thought back to the small weathered cottage that Madame White called home.

"My Lady . . . look at the sheep," Annalee said, as she pointed up at the edge of the cliff.

"Those sheep belong to Thurston Moxley, and it means that we are almost ready to make our way into Cobb Cove."

The women stood on tip-toes and leaned over the railing as far as they could to see the mouth of the cove. As the ship began making the turn, Annalee reached for her sister's hands and jumped up and down with excitement.

"A new adventure for us all," cried Ella. "It will be wonderful won't it, Annalee?"

Annalee raked her teeth across her bottom lip and looked up at Gautier for reassurance.

"There will be many things that you will find in common with your home at Featherstone Castle and many things that are different. Hopefully, you will come to love Black Thistle as much as I have," offered Gautier.

Hearing Hugh speaking to the captain, Gautier excused himself and went to join them.

Men scurried about readying the ship for its arrival. Petula listened to the men shouting as she took in the view of the small harbor. At the sudden sound of boots behind her, Petula stepped back from the bulwark and turned to find Krega and his men standing before her.

"Lady Petula," Krega said, as he and his men bowed. "We have seen you safely to Alltree, and it is time for us to leave you and return to Crownnail."

"I thank you again for your courage in defending me," replied Petula.

"It was our honor to do so."

"Will I ever see you again?"

"If fate requires it, we will see you again."

He could see a flicker of fear in her eyes until she bravely smiled to hide it from him. Trying to comfort her, he took her hand in his own.

"Lady Petula, I find that Lord Gautier is a good and honest man. I know that you can trust him, and he will do his best to keep you safe. Rely on his advice and Lord Heinrich's. They will guide you, but remember, there are those that may try to take advantage of you and your station. If you are ever in danger, you need only call my name. I will come to your aide."

Confused, Petula watched Krega remove a strip of leather from around his neck. Dangling from it was a small silver griffin's claw clutching a smooth red stone.

"If ever your life is in danger, crush this stone and call my name. Hang the empty griffin's claw around your neck, and I will find you."

Krega dropped the bobble into the palm of her hand and closed her fingers around it. He could see the start of tears filling her eyes, and leaned down to kiss the top of her head.

"That kiss was from your father and mother. Now, go ready yourself to greet Lord Heinrich."

* * *

The loud crack of the gangplank against the dock announced their arrival. Gautier stood waiting for Petula as she and her handmaids slowly walked toward him.

"Petula, you look lovely. Take my arm, and I will make sure you don't fall," smiled Gautier. "Are you ready?"

Giving him a nod as she grasped onto his arm, she took in the view before her. Several men stood about holding the reins of horses. Standing alone, a woman with hair the color of flax looked up. Her stare made Petula tremble. Gautier quickly placed his other hand over hers.

"My dear Petula, there is no need to be afraid. They are all here to welcome you to Alltree."

Feeling comforted by his voice, she noticed a tall man with dark shoulder length hair approaching the base of the plank. He was dressed in black with a long slate colored tunic trimmed in gold braid that hung to the top of his black knee-high boots. He stood with his hands behind his back and had a pleasing smile. Looking down for a moment to secure her footing from the plank to the dock, she nervously looked up to see him now standing before her.

"Lady Petula, may I present my brother, Lord Gerwig Heinrich."

"Lord Heinrich, I am honored to meet you," Petula softly said, as she made a deep curtsey.

Gerwig bent down and gently took her glove covered hands to help her stand.

"Lady Petula, I welcome you to Alltree Island. It is an honor to finally meet you. In your father's correspondence, he told me that you are fond of horses."

"I am very fond of horses and of riding."

"Then, I hope you will be pleased with my gift."

Commander Reginald stepped forward holding the reins of a dappled grey mare with a black mane and tail. As he handed them to Gerwig, he could tell that she was taken aback by his appearance. It was a common occurrence for ladies to turn their head away from him. He was somewhat used to it, but he wished that people would one day look beyond his disfigured appearance.

"My Lady, I may not be pleasing to look upon, but I am gentle as a breeze to those that I protect," Reginald said, as he knelt and bowed his head before her. "Lady Petula, I pledge my service to you. I will protect you with my life."

Petula removed her glove and placed her hand upon Reginald's bowed head.

"Commander, I accept your pledge of service and protection. I am truly honored by it. Please stand, you need never kneel before me. You are the sword that stands beside me, and I will never place my sword at my feet, in battle or in peace."

Reginald stood and looked briefly upon Lady Petula's face before he bowed his head and backed away. He was overwhelmed by the words she had spoken. Silently, he vowed he would serve honorably as the sword of her protection. Anyone that tried to harm her would feel the blade of his sword the moment before their death.

Petula suddenly felt the nudging of the mare's nose.

"I see that she has introduced herself," laughed Gerwig. "I hope you like my gift."

"My Lord, thank you. She is beautiful."

"What shall you name her?"

Petula tilted her head and stroked the nose of her new mare. After kissing her nose, she said, "Luna is her name. She is a silver moon surrounded by the dark night."

"You have chosen a beautiful name," replied Gerwig. "Let's get you up on Luna's back and make our way to Black Thistle."

He helped Petula secure her position on Luna's back and mounted his own horse. Taking the reins, he looked over his shoulder at his brother.

"Gautier, the commander will escort us back to the castle. Will you see after her ladies and the wagon?"

"I will, My Lord."

Gerwig nudged his silver stallion with the heels of his boots and slowly made his way from the dock with Petula by his side. He was happy he had chosen her. Now, he had to wait for her to choose him.

Gautier saw Velsa the minute they entered the cove and dreaded having to deal with her. As he helped Ella and Annalee into the wagon, he felt her presence behind him.

"You didn't need to come all the way out here," said Gautier without turning around.

"I wanted to greet you. It has been so long since I have seen you. Did you have a good voyage?" asked Velsa.

Gautier stepped to the rear of the wagon to try and keep their conversation private.

"It was uneventful."

After hearing his own false words, he looked up to see Krega and his men flying overhead. They circled the ship twice and headed for home. Distracted by the sight of them, he didn't hear Velsa speaking to him. When he felt her stroke his face, he drew back away from her.

"Where were you?" she asked. "I was speaking to you, and it was as if you didn't hear me."

"Velsa, I am tired. I have not had a good night's rest since setting foot on the Lucinda May. Go back to the castle. Wait for me there. We will speak later. I have work to do here."

Velsa could hear the girls whispering, and she was embarrassed by his response. Without giving it another thought, she vanished.

* * *

"This is not going well," screamed Velsa as she paced back and forth in front of the hearth in her bedchamber. "What has happened to my beloved Gautier? Who has bewitched him? Who has turned him against me?"

A rap at her door calmed her frantic mind, and she hurried to the door. Swinging the door wide, she was greeted by Gautier's solemn expression. Taking his hand, she felt him flinch as she led him inside to a chair by the hearth.

"I am sorry if I upset you," Velsa whispered, as she knelt at Gautier's feet and cradled her face in the palms of his hands.

"It was meant to be a formal greeting for Lady Petula, and it was not your place to wait for me at the dock," he replied. "I had responsibilities to fulfill to Lord Larchmont and my brother. Lady Petula is far from home and surrounded by strangers. She may be my sister soon, and I wish to be a source of strength for her."

"For her? A source of strength for her? What about me?"

"What about you? You hardly need strength from me. You could simply snap your fingers and have whatever you want. I have seen you turn ale to berry wine at Gerwig's table when you thought no one was looking."

Standing abruptly, she turned her back on him and crossed her arms over her chest. Feeling she had made things worse, she quickly faced him and took hold of his hands.

"Do you think that is what I have done to you? Do you think I have cast a spell to make you love me?"

Gautier's brows furrowed, and he pulled his hands free of hers.

"When have I said that I love you? I cannot remember saying the words to you."

"That is true. You have not said them, but I know you feel them in your heart. You are simply waiting until your brother is wed before you profess your love for me. I understand the order of things."

Gautier swallowed his bitter thoughts and took a deep breath to calm his temper.

"Too often, your words are spoken without thinking. I find them unsettling. It is true; we have a history of sorts."

Feeling the sting of his description of their time together, she tried to ignore it.

"We do have a lovely history."

Gautier raised his hand to quiet her.

"I am not here to speak of what we have or have not shared. I am here to ask you to accompany me to this evening's festivities as my brother introduces Lady Petula to the people of Black Thistle. Please be on your best behavior."

At first his words cut Velsa to the core, but when she heard his invitation, she quickly forgot them.

"I would love . . . Yes, I will accompany you to the festivities this evening. I will choose something beautiful to wear. I want you to be proud of me."

"My brother has a request. Do not wear Black Thistle's colors. He has given Petula a gown the color of our thistles, and she will be the center of attention tonight. He wants nothing to distract from her arrival. Choose a gown the color of the sky at noon or of the amber sunset. Please, do not anger my brother. For if you do, you anger me."

"As you wish. I will not wear purple or green."

"I will leave you to your preparations."

Velsa watched as he left her chamber and knew for certain that something had caused the sudden distance in their relationship. Since she hadn't changed, something or someone had caused him to change. For now, she would set that aside and focus on preparing for the party.

* * *

As Velsa walked through the dimly lit hallway toward the Great Hall, she nervously pulled on the delicate lace that rested just off her shoulders. She had chosen an amber gown that she found went perfectly with her hair. The addition of the corset tied tightly with gold ribbons accented her tiny waist while exposing just the tops of her plump breasts. After Gautier's suggestion of a gown the color of an amber sunset, she thought it to be an excellent choice.

The music was the first thing she heard as she approached the doors to the Great Hall. The thought of dancing with Gautier brought a smile to her face, but it quickly faded upon hearing her name whispered in anger. Leaning toward the shadows, she quietly crept towards the open doorway to listen.

"Put her in her place or I will."

"I have no control over her."

"You have more than enough power to handle her. She has overstepped her bounds. She is not part of this family, and she never will be. You have dallied with her far too long. She clearly is not your fated mate. I order you to end it."

"I believe the end is well on its way."

"Make sure that it is."

Stunned after recognizing the voices of Gerwig and Gautier, tears welled in Velsa's eyes. Gautier was truly done with her.

Why now, she thought? We have been happy with one another for so long.

Gathering her composure, she vanished the tears from her eyes. Determined to enjoy the party, she raised her chin as an evil thought crossed her mind. Suddenly, the amber gown she wore didn't seem fitting for her last party at Black Thistle Castle. She needed something more festive and much more dramatic. Trying to keep from laughing, Velsa waved her hand and her gown changed color.

"Now, let's have some fun at this party," she smirked.

Gautier had begun to raise his goblet for a much needed taste of ale when he heard the gasp. The room was suddenly quiet as Velsa slowly made her way toward him. Her once-perfect amber gown had been replaced with a gown of crimson satin. The corset was low and tight to allow the fullness of her breasts to be enjoyed by all that were brave enough to look. At her neck hung a heart-shaped ruby tied on a black velvet ribbon.

"Woman, have you no shame?" Gautier uttered, through clenched teeth.

"Since this is my last party, I thought I should dress the part that everyone thinks I am playing, your whore," whispered Velsa.

Gautier slammed his goblet down before he grabbed her arm and forcibly walked her from the room. Yanking her arm from Gautier's hold, she vanished to her bedchamber. It wasn't long before he burst through the door to confront her.

"Have you lost your mind?"

"Gautier, what did you expect me to do? I was angry after I heard you and your brother talking. He has ordered you to end it; however, I believe that you were well on your way of doing just that before he demanded it."

"Gerwig has ordered it, and it is true that I have been thinking of doing the same for some time. I find I need my freedom from you. I have waited for the sign that we were meant to be united, and it has never presented itself. You know that to be true."

Velsa began to cry as she tore at the laces of her corset and pulled it from her body. Dropping it to the floor, she took a much needed breath.

"It isn't our time. It is your brother's time. You know the order of things."

"Fate is not prejudiced by the order of things. If we were meant to be together, fate would have made it known. It has been silent, Velsa. It has been silent for years."

"Can we give it more time? Please, can we give it more time?"

"Time will not fix it. I find our time is over. I release you and ask that you willingly release me. To go against this now is wrong. It would be against my brother's order and of fate's desire. We are finished."

Velsa sank to the floor wrapping her arms around her waist. Looking up at Gautier, she felt the sting of tears that fell from her eyes.

"Please, it isn't over! Gautier, I still love you."

Her pain pulled at his heart, but he couldn't let it bend his resolve.

"You must be gone by week's end. If you need . . ."

Before he could finish speaking, she had vanished.

* * *

Velsa stood naked in the darkness of the Black Thistle Forest after ripping her crimson dress to shreds. She had coughed and gagged on bitter tasting words that spewed uncontrollably from her mouth. Exhausted from her fit of rage, she wiped the tears from her face and vowed to never shed another tear.

"Lord Gautier, you will pay for your betrayal. It will not be today or tomorrow, but it will come. When it does, you will beg me to stop the pain, and I will walk away laughing," she shouted, as she willingly opened her heart to the darkness that surrounded her.

* * *

The space was cramped and nothing like her chambers in Black Thistle Castle. She hadn't conjured a cottage in years, and she didn't have the energy to make it any larger. Her anger at Gautier's surprise declaration had exhausted her, and after returning with her belongings, she had collapsed on her cot.

"Now what do I do?" she sighed and started pulling the leather binding from her braid. "What is this?" She quickly moved to take advantage of the candlelight. "Something dreadful has happened to my hair!"

She unraveled the woven strands and pulled them up toward the light. They had completely lost their golden color. She cupped the grey lifeless strands in her hand while stroking them with her fingers. She had heard of witches that had let anger take control of their appearance.

Did my anger cause this? Surely, one little temper tantrum would not have caused my hair to change color.

She tried to remember the last time she had been angry and why. The moments were more than she could count on one hand, and the reasons were hardly worth remembering.

Could the stars believe I have been angry too often?

Perplexed by this sudden change, Velsa reached for her book of spells. Flipping through the pages, she soon realized there wasn't anything within the pages that could explain what had happened. Placing her beloved book back onto her small table, she began searching for her sphere. Fancy gowns, slippers, and hair ribbons littered everything. Tossing them to the floor, she rummaged through her belongings until she finally found it.

Holding it up to let the flickering candlelight shine through it, she whispered a few words and watched as a vision of herself standing in the forest was revealed. Her shoulders tensed as she heard the curses that flew from her lips. She winced as she witnessed herself tearing her crimson gown to shreds. It wasn't until she heard herself curse the stars that her hair began to change color. She had done the unthinkable and blamed the stars for her loss of Gautier. As the sphere darkened, Velsa slumped to the floor, and her sphere tumbled from her hand.

"I did this to myself. I will never be forgiven," she scolded herself.

Sitting amongst the mounds of silk and brocade, she brought her knees to her chest. Wrapping her arms around her legs, she began to rock back and forth as a gentle whimper escaped her lips. With each breath she took, the whimpering grew louder. Her body flinched as the whimpering became painful gasps for air. Struggling to breath, she felt dizzy, and her vision began to blur. Unable to see, she closed her eyes and begged the stars for forgiveness.

"You ask us for forgiveness? You must be worthy to receive forgiveness from the stars. Do you not remember cursing us? We wait for your atonement. Only then will you have forgiveness," a stern voice replied to her request.

Looking up, she tried to see what she felt hovering above her head.

"You don't understand; you have taken the one thing from me that Gautier finds beautiful."

"My dear Velsa, I hear vanity instead of an apology. I fear you are traveling a path that leads you further away from the goodness you once possessed."

Frustrated, Velsa stood with her hands clenched so tightly that she could feel her nails digging into her palms. She was teetering on losing control.

"Think before you speak. One more word of profanity, and we will leave you forever."

Velsa could feel heat racing from her hands up her arms. Sparks began to burst from her skin as she arched her back trying to stop the pain.

"Then, leave me forever if that is what you desire. It makes no difference to me. I have no need of your scorn. Be gone! Be gone with you!"

The sudden pain in Velsa's arms was unbearable. Pointing her hands at the hearth, she let the sparks fly from her fingertips as she tried to relieve the burning sensation. She could feel the moment the spirit of the stars left her cottage. As it did, a cold darkness entered in its place. It wrapped its arms around her shoulders and took away the pain. The comfort was something she had never felt before, and she leaned back into its cool grasp.

"You need not feel any pain. I am here for you," a calm voice whispered in her ear.

Velsa felt something lift her from her feet and carry her to her cot. As she was gently placed down upon the thin cushion, she tried to see what had offered her comfort, but she could find no one.

"Who is there?"

"My name is Balgair. I heard your cries through the trees that surround your cottage."

"Balgair?"

"Yes, I will be your friend if you will allow it. I am able to help you if you help me in return. Now, you need only rest. We will speak in the morning after you have rested."

Velsa could feel a hand against her eyes before a calm darkness offered her sleep.

* * *

Balgair had spent the night in Velsa's cottage watching her sleep. He had listened to her talk as she fought her nightmares, watched her toss and turn within her coverlet, and even quieted her wretched snoring. Something had unsettled her, and he had felt it long before he had entered her cottage. From a distance, he had seen the torn bits of red satin scattered about the forest. As he approached them, the energy that surrounded them was thick and filled with dark magic. It was a sign that evil was attempting to creep through the crack in her defenses. He wondered if she had let it. If so, it was only a matter of time before it owned all of her.

Leaning back in the only chair in her cottage with his feet propped up on a milking stool, he planned what he hoped would be a long term alliance. He had been looking for a witch that would provide him occasional assistance, and he believed he had found her. As a collector, his only goal was to protect himself by gaining as many powers as he could from others. It didn't matter to him what creature offered them willingly or before their death. If they came from a well-made bargain, it served them both. He would collect any power that he found useful. He believed an alliance with the witch would be beneficial to him and to her.

The first inkling Balgair noticed that Velsa was about to wake was the flutter of her eyelashes. Removing his feet from the stool, he sat hunched over with his elbows on his knees and his chin resting on his fists. Prepared for an outburst, he calmed the air around her and waited to greet her.

With a soft moan, Velsa opened her eyes and began brushing her tangled hair from her face. Wiping the sleep from her eyes, she pushed herself up from her cot and had both feet on the floor before she saw Balgair staring at her. Confused as to why a stranger was staring at her, she raised her hand to protect herself. A few meager sparks did nothing more than sizzle at the tips of her fingers. Shaking her head, she looked at her hands and then up at Balgair.

"There is no need for any of that nonsense. I'm not here to hurt you. You might say that I have kept you from hurting yourself," he laughed, as he stood and stepped toward her. "We have much to talk about. Before we do; however, you need to freshen up a bit. Choose something to wear from the items you have cluttering the floor of your cottage. I will step outside to give you some privacy. Once you are ready, we will talk."

As Balgair opened the door to step outside, Velsa stood and looked about the dimly lit room. All she could remember was leaving Black Thistle Castle, the dreadful encounter she had with a star spirit, and the unbearable pain in her arms. As she bent down to pick up a crumpled gown, she vaguely remembered hearing a man's voice. It had been strong and comforting at the same time.

Still unsure of what to make of the silver-haired stranger's sudden arrival, she donned the simple gown and smoothed the wrinkles away with her hands. Looking at her unsightly grey locks, she untangled them the best she could and loosely braided them. Gathering up the clothing that made her think of Gautier, she caused them to vanish. Spying her slippers under the table, she drew them to her and had them securely on her feet as she opened the door.

"You may as well enter. It appears you will even if I don't want you here," she fussed, as she turned her back on him and plopped down on her cot.

Leaving the door open, he dragged the chair closer to her.

"Since you probably don't remember my name, I will introduce myself again. My name is Balgair. You may have heard of me or heard that I am a threat." He saw her draw back and furrow her brow. "Let me reassure you. I'm not here to hurt you."

"You have me at a disadvantage. I do not recall hearing your name."

"You might have heard of the Silver Fox or The Collector."

Velsa had thought the tales of the Silver Fox had only been rumors. She had never met a vampire that was as powerful as a witch, and it was unsettling.

He saw the recognition in her eyes as she clenched her fists in her lap.

"I see that you have heard of me. Now, let's talk about what you can do for me."

"What could I possibly do for a vampire, or better yet, why would I want to do anything for you?"

Impressed that she had taken the time to discover he was a vampire, he sat down facing her.

"I would imagine that you could do many things for a vampire. I'll let you decide after you hear my proposal."

"If you must continue, get on with it. I have much to do today."

"I am in need of occasional potions to assist me in my endeavors. I would assume that you are in need of rare herbs, spices, and gemstones that are not found on this island."

He could see by her expression that he had peeked her interest.

"My desire to collect unusual powers causes me to travel to distant and exotic islands. On these exotic islands, I have found many rare items that would be useful to a witch such as yourself."

"Are you implying that a trade be made. I give you potions, and you give me rare items in return."

"I propose we enter into a union that will benefit both of us."

"You have presented an intriguing proposal. It would benefit me greatly; however, I would have one condition before I could agree."

"What would that be?"

"No potion would be used to deliberately cause harm to anyone. My white magic nor I will allow it."

"Agreed."

"How shall we make this binding? A Binding Potion? Blood?"

"I give you my word. There is no need to draw blood. I believe that I have shown that I can be trusted."

"Your word is enough. I give you mine in return, but do not betray me. Betraying a witch can be extremely painful."

"Betraying a vampire can be just as painful and often deadly."

Uncomfortable with his threat, Velsa felt a cold shiver race up her spine.

Balgair stood and walked to the door. Turning, he offered her a smile and a gracious bow.

"I must leave you. A ship waits for me in the harbor. When I return, I will bring you the gifts I have promised."

Before she could reply, he had vanished leaving a silver mist in his place.

Chapter 6

Gautier took great relief in the fact that the whispering about Velsa's bold entrance had finally stopped. It was all he could do to force himself to face those that had been in attendance that evening. He was sure they still saw the look of embarrassment upon his face, and it pained him.

The first time he had brought her to the castle, his brother had voiced his dislike for her actions and her opinions. He had not listened to his brother's warnings, and hoped that the long awaited bolt of heat would present itself, proving his brother wrong. So, he waited and continued the relationship. Now that he had found the white wolf, he realized how selfish he had been. He had ignored Velsa's feelings and hurt her terribly. The moment of their undoing was brittle at best; however, it was done.

Closing the door to his chamber, he headed for the Command Center. He needed the distraction of the daily routine with the army. He needed to hear the clashing of blades and the grunts of his men to take his thoughts from her. As he passed what had been her chamber door, he heard it open. Fearing to turn around and see her standing there, he took a deep breath and waited to hear her voice. Continued silence caused him to look over his shoulder. Finding Velsa's maid, Faye, with a bundle of bedding in her arms, he exhaled.

"Good morning, Lord Gautier," she offered, as she pulled the door closed.

"Has she left much behind?" asked Gautier.

"Her possessions are gone. She has left nothing." Stepping back away from the door, she continued. "Do you wish to see for yourself?"

"No, that is not required. Don't let me keep you from your duties."

With a sigh of relief, Gautier quickly turned and headed for the white witch's chamber. He knew that Velsa's chamber had been full of her belongings when his harsh words had caused her to vanish. That meant she had returned to the castle to retrieve them. Her comings and goings needed to be stopped, and he needed to be completely free of her. For that, he needed her help.

The witch, Derora, had come to Alltree Island just after their father had moved their mother into Black Thistle Castle. A strange illness had caused their mother to be confined to bed for several moons, and Derora had provided a tonic that had cured her. In appreciation, he had moved her from her tiny cottage in Cobb Cove to the castle, giving her a bedchamber with an adjoining chamber for her books and herbs. After learning she was more than a healer, he put his trust in her to protect the castle and its people. She had served him well and continued her service even after his passing.

Gautier could see the door to Derora's library was open, and he could hear her humming a familiar tune. Before he could reach the doorway, he heard her beckoning him to join her.

"What brings you to my little sanctuary? Are you in need of more magic lessons?" she laughed.

He was greeted by her warm smile and outstretched arms. She had been his teacher when it was discovered that he possessed magical powers, and she had kept him away from the temptation of dark magic. After his mother's passing, and the seemingly unending period of grief felt by his father, she had willingly taken on the role of his mother. She had taught him to respect others, show kindness and compassion, always act honorably, and trust his instincts. His instincts told him he needed her help.

"My DeDe, it is good to see you."

"I see that you are troubled. What can I do to ease your burden?"

"I need your counsel, DeDe. I am sure you have heard the gossip about Velsa's shameful display. She humiliated herself and me in front of everyone."

"I have heard some gossip."

"I have ended it, and it ended badly. What Velsa and I shared is over."

He hung his head in shame, but Derora placed her finger under his chin to make him look at her.

"Gautier, it was time for it to end. Fate has other plans for you. I have seen it."

"You know of my white wolf?"

"Yes, I have seen your white wolf. She has hidden her secret for many years, and she continues to hide her secret from many that would harm her. She fears you will expose it. Gautier, she needs your protection."

"I know that she is my fated one. I have felt it, and I long for the day we can always be together."

"I must warn you to go slowly and be patient. Let her and her wolf trust you. When she does, love will surely follow." Seeing him purse his lips, she tapped his nose with her finger. "Your brother has found his mate. Now, go secure yours. I will do what is necessary to protect Black Thistle. You need not worry about Velsa coming to the castle."

Gautier wrapped his arms around Derora and lifted her up above his head as he danced around the table letting her laughter fill his senses. For now, the worry was gone, and his thoughts were only of his white wolf and no other.

* * *

The ride to Woods Village took him through the Black Thistle Forest, across Whistler's River, and past the Old Mill. It wasn't until he crossed the wooden bridge over Wood Cutter's Water that he noticed the sun was beginning to rise, and he felt his heartbeat quicken. He had been careful to leave the Black Thistle markings behind. They seemed to draw unwanted attention to himself and others that were with him. He remembered Derora's counsel, and he felt it might put Madame White in danger if he had worn them.

As he made his way through Woods Village, he noticed a lad leaving Big John's Market carrying a basket of apples. Feeling his stomach rumble, he called out for the lad to stop. Dismounting his horse, he approached the lad.

"Could you spare a couple of apples?" asked Gautier, as he retrieved his leather pouch from his hip. "I would gladly pay for them. It has been a long ride, and I find that I am hungry."

The lad looked at the apples and then at the coins. Nodding, he set the basket down. Choosing two of the biggest apples, he placed them in Gautier's open palm and retrieved the coins.

"I hope this doesn't get you into any trouble with your mother."

"We made a fair trade, sir. She will be pleased with the coins."

Rubbing the apple first on the sleeve of his tunic, he then took a bite. It snapped from the pressure of his teeth, and its sweet juice filled his mouth. Looking down at the other apple, he had an idea. Tucking it into the neck of his tunic, he finished his apple as he walked back to his horse.

To avoid being seen, he took the less travelled path through the trees and along the edge of the cliff that overlooked the sea. With her small cottage finally in sight, he dismounted his horse, tethered him to a sturdy bush, and quietly walked toward the porch of her cottage. Retrieving the apple from his tunic, he placed it on the edge of the porch and hide among some bushes in hopes of seeing her.

It wasn't long before Madame White walked out onto her porch with a basket over her arm. As she latched her door, he saw her notice the apple. He was delighted when he saw her snatch it from the porch and take a bite. Staying out of sight, he saw her throw the core into a bucket and jump from the porch to the path that would take her to the village. Not taking his eyes off her, he noticed her fondness for the wildflowers that lined the path, and he had another idea.

Once she was out of sight, he carefully snapped a few stalks of the prettiest flowers that he had seen her admire. With flowers in hand, he made his way back to her cottage and took his place on her porch to wait for her return.

* * *

Since the absence of Lord Gautier in Woods Village, Kayleigh had enjoyed the quiet solitude while watching the morning sunrise. She no longer looked over her shoulder for him or his horse in the stable on her way to Big John's Market. At the nagging of her wolf, she had even relented and given herself over to her for a few moonlit runs. Her life seemed to be getting back to normal, and she was relieved.

With her basket full of sweet cake and berry jam, she readied herself for a walk into the village. The weather had improved, and she was in need of seeds to start her garden. Deciding it was warm enough to leave her shawl on the wooden peg, she hurried out the door. While securing the latch, she noticed something red out of the corner of her eye. At the far end of the porch sat a single apple. The only apple orchard on the island belonged to Fallon Castle.

Had someone discovered who she was? Was this a warning?

Warning or not, she was tired of running. Without giving it another thought, she picked up the red delight and took a bite. It was crisp, juicy, and just as sweet as she had remembered. A bit of sadness filled her heart as she thought about her home and her parents. She had not laid eyes on Fallon Castle since seeing her mother standing on her balcony. Preferring to keep only happiness in her heart, she let the sadness drift away as she tossed what remained of her apple into her empty water bucket and jumped from the porch.

The path from her cottage to the village was lined with colorful wildflowers. The gentle sea breeze caused their buds and blooms to sway along with the tall grass that nestled at their roots. Taken by the movement, she slowed and let her fingers linger over the petals of the yellow Buttercups and red Poppies. They had always been her favorites, and she had eagerly awaited their arrival. Now that the warm weather had arrived, she would have the pleasure of their beauty to brighten her day.

Kayleigh could see the village square had become crowded with men and wagons. Since the ship had docked in Woods Bay, a steady stream of wagons had made their way to and from the ship carrying supplies and people to the village. Noticing several people huddled outside of the market, her curiosity made her hurry her step.

"No, I didn't see them. I was told by someone from Primrose Pond," the tall man snapped. "He is reliable. He rarely forwards gossip."

"Keep your children close and under a watchful eye," the man next to him offered. "They are known to eat children."

Confused, Kayleigh entered the market to find Big John polishing his counter.

"Good morning to you, Madame White," said Big John.

"It is a good morning. Do you know of what the men speak?" she asked.

"Someone is spreading tales of seeing griffins in the sky."

"Griffins . . . here . . . on Alltree? My father spoke of them once in a bedtime story. He said that they lived in a castle deep in a stone mountain far from here. Do you believe the tale?"

"I have seen many a strange thing in my lifetime. I don't doubt that unbelievable creatures exist in someone's mind.

After a night of too much ale, I have seen some things I was glad had left me by morning."

Kayleigh laughed and sat her basket on the counter. Unwrapping the cloth, she showed him what she hoped to trade.

"The sweet cake is fresh from my hearth. Smeared with berry jam, it would be a heavenly addition to someone's table."

"It would indeed."

"In trade, I am in need of seeds for my garden and some eggs."

"My sweet tooth can hardly wait to have a slice. Help yourself to the seeds. Madame, you have found my weakness. With trades such as this, your garden will soon be overflowing."

Kayleigh smiled when she saw him carefully put the cake and jam out of sight. Looking for the seeds, she noticed a basket full of apples.

"Someone left an apple on my porch this morning. Do you know who left it?"

"Do you have a secret admirer?"

"I hope not. It would not be proper and would draw unwanted gossip."

"I did not mean to offend you. It was only a joke. Please excuse my ill humor?"

Kayleigh nodded and gave him a weak smile.

"It didn't get there on its own. Someone must have put it there."

"Young Penn was in early to buy apples for his mother. Maybe he left one on your porch on the way home."

"I did help his mother with her garden. If I see the young man, I will ask him and offer my thanks. It was a delightful surprise."

Gathering up her seed packets and four eggs, she set them on the counter. Big John placed them in her basket along with a small linen pouch of flour.

"A little extra to help you make another sweet cake."

"Big John, you spoil me. Enjoy your cake and have a good day."

"Come back soon."

He had already bent down to where he had stowed the cake before she had managed to leave the market.

As Kayleigh made her way back to her cottage, she noticed Penn helping his friend, Adam, wheeling a cart full of soiled straw. Quickening her step, she called out to the young man.

"Penn . . . Penn, might I have a word?"

Hearing his name, they stopped to wait for her.

"Madame White, do you need help?"

"I wanted to thank you for the apple you placed on my porch this morning. It was a delightful surprise."

"It was not me, Madame."

"Big John told me you left the market with apples. I assumed it was you that left it on my porch."

"It could have been the man that left it."

"What man?"

"A tall man with shiny boots bought two apples from me for a very good price. He said that he was hungry. Even though I returned with two less apples, my mother was pleased to see the coin I gave her."

"I'm sure of it."

Feeling certain she knew who had left it on her porch, she wanted to defer any gossip the boys might decide to pass on to others.

"It was probably Tilly that left it. I help her with her laundry, and she always leaves me something in payment for my time."

"She does the same to my mother, but she often leaves us onions instead of apples."

Penn wrinkled his nose, as did Adam.

"Well, I had better be on my way. I'm sorry I delayed you."

Waving to the boys she headed for the path that would take her home. She could feel her heart racing as she hurried past the wildflowers. As she approached her cottage, she saw someone sitting on the edge of her porch. Coming to a sudden stop, she was certain that the sound of her boots upon the path must have been heard. After looking about to see if anyone was watching, she slowly walked toward her cottage. There before her stood Gautier holding a handful of buttercups and poppies.

* * *

The warmth of the sun had caused a soft blush to cover her cheeks, and Gautier couldn't take his eyes off of her. As she slowly walked toward him, he found himself counting each step she took until she stood before him.

"Someone left an apple on my porch. Was it you?" asked Kayleigh.

She had not even offered him a hint of a smile, and he feared he had wronged her.

"I had two apples and no one to share them with," replied Gautier.

He saw her tilt her head as she tried to determine if he told the truth.

"If you meant to share it with someone, why did you abandon it on my porch?"

"I thought to surprise you."

"And the flowers, were they to be a surprise too?"

Gautier felt his head spinning, and he could tell that she wasn't going to make this easy for him. He had never let a woman have the upper hand before, and try as he may to gain control, he found she had him floundering for the right words to say.

"I saw how much you admired the blooms, and I thought they would brighten your table."

He heard her gasp and saw fire in her eyes.

"You saw me? Where were you?" she snapped. "Were you spying on me as you sat hiding in the bushes?"

She backed away from him and stepped up onto her porch. Staring down at him, she waited for an answer.

What else can go wrong? This isn't how I planned our meeting, he thought.

"I am sorry. I have made a mess of this. I thought only to make you happy. I should have made myself known. I was foolish. Please forgive me." Not knowing what else to do, he got down on his knees and held the flowers up to her. "I beg you to forgive me."

Seeing him, a Lord of Black Thistle Castle, on his knees caught her by surprise, and she started to laugh.

"Does this mean I am forgiven?"

"It is against my better judgement, but yes, you are forgiven. Get off your knees at once and hand me those flowers before they wilt in your hands."

As she took the flowers from him, her hand brushed against his, and she felt the same warmth she had felt before. Trying to ignore it, she headed for her door.

"Wait here while I put the flowers in some water."

He watched her enter her cottage and immediately felt her absence. Waiting the few moments it took for her to return was agonizing. He heard a soft sigh pass over his lips as he saw her step back out onto the porch carrying two wooden mugs.

"I thought you might be thirsty."

She handed him a cup and sat down on the porch letting her legs dangle over the edge.

"May I?" He pointed to the spot next to her and saw her nod.

Sitting down, he took a drink from the cup and tried to organize his thoughts before he spoke.

"I don't know how to say this, and my words are not meant to offend you in any way. So, I will just say what is on my mind."

"I'm listening."

"I know your secret."

Kayleigh turned her face away from him and felt tears begin to fill her eyes. It had been her greatest fear that someone would discover it, and now, they had.

"I know your secret, and you have my word that I will not expose it to anyone."

"How did you find out?"

"I am not an ordinary man. I have been given the gift of magic."

She turned back to search his face for any sign that he was lying and saw nothing but a serious expression staring back at her.

"I knew the day we met that you had a secret, and I have seen the beautiful secret that you have kept hidden."

"You have seen my wolf?"

"I have seen her in the moonlight, and she is beautiful."

"I have been so happy here alone in the village. If others find out about me, I will be forced to leave. I don't know where I would go."

"I told you; you have my word. I will not reveal your secret."

"What else do you know about me?"

"I know that your true name is not Madame White. Is there more I should know?"

"I may as well tell you all of it. Come inside where others cannot hear my story."

Kayleigh stood, and Gautier followed her into her cottage not knowing what to expect.

* * *

He had listened to her talk about her home at Fallon Castle, her love for her late mother and father, and the horrible day she was banished from the castle by her father. It wasn't until she mentioned how things might have been different if she had accepted the man's offer of assistance that he realized he had been the one to offer her the ride home. Even then, fate had tried to unite them. As she finished her story, he had yet to hear her true name.

Without waiting another moment, he asked, "Will you say your name for me. I have yet to hear your true name."

"My name is Kayleigh. I was once Lady Kayleigh of Fallon Castle. Now, I am only Kayleigh. To others here in this village, I am Madame White."

Her name was music to his ears. It was the most beautiful name he had ever heard.

"You are not merely Kayleigh; you are Kayleigh and the White Wolf."

And, you are my Kayleigh, he thought.

As she sat with her hands in her lap after talking for hours, he knew that she was exhausted, but she had surprised him by asking to hear his own story. Not wanting their time together to end, he willingly told her everything about Black Thistle Castle, his family, his journey to Crownnail to retrieve Lady Petula, how he discovered his gift of magic, his relationship with Velsa, and how it ended. He found her sudden laughter over his description of Velsa's gown to be delightful, and he knew he would never tire of hearing that delightful sound.

With the realization that he needed to see after his horse, Gautier stood and stepped behind his chair. Leaning against its back he gathered his courage.

"Would you like to walk with me to see after my horse? I find I am not ready to leave you yet."

"A walk would be nice. Is your horse far?"

"No, he is tied to some bushes just beyond your cottage."

As she retrieved her shawl, he opened the door for her knowing they had bound themselves forever with each other's secrets.

* * *

Gautier woke long before the sun's light had pooled on the wooden floor of his room at the tavern. He had spent the night replaying every moment he had spent with Kayleigh over and over in his mind, and he couldn't wait to see her again. Now, every moment that passed without seeing her smile or hearing the sound of her voice was pure torture for him. It was all he could do to keep himself from shouting her name and telling everyone he had found the one person that would make his life complete.

As he paced back and forth in front of the tiny window, he suddenly realized that he was nervous. He found it odd because he had never been nervous a day in his life. Just thinking of Kayleigh had him doubting his masculinity. After all, he had fallen on his knees before her to beg for her forgiveness, and he would gladly do it again if he found his words ever hurt her.

Peering out the window, he saw Big John crossing the square. Letting his door slam a little too loudly, he took the stairs of the tavern as swiftly as his boots would allow him. Looking about for Madame Opal, the tavern keeper, he saw her coming from the kitchen with a plate of hot food in each hand. He waved three coins in front of her eyes and dropped them safely into her apron pocket.

"I'll be needing the room for another night," he said, as he maneuvered through the tables and chairs on his way to the door.

"What's the hurry? Something sweet caught your eye?" she asked.

He could hear the men laughing, but it didn't bother him. With his back to the door, he gave them a big grin before hurrying out the door.

As Gautier entered the market, he nodded his greeting to Big John. His eyes were already scanning the crates and baskets for apples as he closed the door. Not seeing any, he offered Big John a look of disappointment.

"I'm looking for more of the apples I bought from the young lad yesterday. Have you any more apples today?"

"There is one more basket in the back. I was just about to bring it out. I'll get it for you," Big John said, as he threw a damp cloth onto the counter."

While he waited for Big John to return, Gautier snatched a few carrots and a large bundle of candles. Hearing Big John struggling with the heavy basket, he sat his items down on the counter and hurried to lend him a hand.

"What brings you out so early this morning. The sun is barely up?" asked Big John.

"I thought while I was here in the village I would offer my help and take some oil to Mr. Brumley for you. After returning from a voyage to Crownnail Island, I know how important the tower's light could be to a ship at sea."

"Crownnail you say. I guess you've heard the rumors?"

"What rumors are those?"

"Some folks around here have been whispering of griffins in the sky. I remember my father telling tales of giant griffins that plucked ships from the sea. He said they came from stone caves on Crownnail Island. Did you see any of the creatures on your voyage?"

Gautier bent down and picked up a couple of apples in each hand and laughed. Deciding not to give credence to the griffin sightings, he played along. After all, the last thing Lord Larchmont would want would be hunters searching Crownnail to try and kill the griffins.

"Between you and me, I did see them, but it was only after fighting to stay alive during a fierce storm that left me face down against the deck of the ship. Who knows if it was real or my exhausted mind playing tricks on me."

"I can't imagine the rumors are true. A creature made from an eagle and lion would surely be something made from a mind clouded by too much ale." Big John laughed and slapped Gautier on the shoulder. "Enough talk of creatures, let me get the oil for you. If we keep talking, the sun will be high in the sky before you can retrieve your horse from the stable."

* * *

The ride to the old tower was an easy one, and the sea breeze had kept him cool from the morning sun. After stowing the oil at the top of the tower, Gautier passed on all the gossip he had heard in the village and all about his voyage to Crownnail. He sat on the stone stoop and listened to Mr. Brumley go on about his memories of his beloved Hilda and how much he missed her. He could see tears fill the old man's eyes as he lovingly spoke about her, and he knew he would feel the same if he ever lost Kayleigh. Seeing the sun had passed beyond midday, Gautier knew it was time for him to go. Leaving Mr. Brumley standing at the gate, Gautier mounted his horse and gave the old man a wave before he headed for Kayleigh's cottage.

He saw the smoke from the chimney long before he saw her cottage. Even though it was completely open to the sea, its view from the road was well protected by a thick crop of trees. After previously taking her home from the tower, he knew exactly where to find the narrow hidden path that led to her door.

Dismounting and tethering his horse, he could smell what he thought was rabbit stew and heard his stomach grumble over missing his morning meal. After untying the cloth sack from the horn of the saddle, he grasped it tightly as he stepped up onto the wooden porch. With a gentle rap upon her door, he nervously waited to hear her voice. Instead, he was surprised as the door opened wide, and he was greeted by her smile.

"You open the door to anyone?" scolded Gautier. "It could have been a thief from the ship anchored in the bay. Who knows what harm he could have caused you."

"I knew it was you. I know your scent." She bit her bottom lip trying not to laugh when she saw his surprised expression. "You forget, I am a wolf, and I do have ways of protecting myself."

"That may be, but a well guided dagger could still do you harm."

"And, the attacker would have his head ripped from his shoulders for his effort. I am not as fragile as you think I am. My wolf has been able to protect me for a very long time."

Gautier took a deep breath. He hated to compare Kayleigh to Velsa, but he had found himself standing before another strong willed woman. One that wasn't afraid to put him in his place.

"It appears that I have a way of saying the wrong thing."

"You speak your mind, and you will find that I do the same. If we spend all of our time seeking forgiveness for our words, we won't have time to enjoy each other."

"You can add wisdom to your list of talents."

He found himself shifting his weight from one foot to the other at a loss for what to do next. Seeing his indecision, Kayleigh stepped out onto the porch.

"Do you like your rabbit stew hot or cold?"

"Hot."

"Then, I suggest you come in before it gets cold."

* * *

They had feasted on rabbit stew, bread fresh from the fire, slices of apples, and sweet berry wine before he had talked her into going for a ride. He assured her he would not take the well-travelled road to keep from being seen and stay on the path along the cliffs that would allow them privacy. With her seated in front of him and her back leaning against his chest, the same heat he had felt before raced up his arms, and he found it calmed his senses. Reaching a small patch of sweet grass that overlooked the sea, Gautier stopped his horse.

"I have a blanket rolled up behind me, would you like to sit and watch the colorful sunset the sky will be offering us soon?"

"I would love to watch the sunset."

He dismounted and gently lifted Kayleigh from his horse's back. After he spread the blanket out on the soft sweet grass, he helped her sit before he took his place beside her. She pulled her knees up to her chest and pulled her shawl around her shoulders careful to grasp it tightly around her knees.

"Gautier, this was a wonderful idea. Watching the sun rise in the morning and set in the evening has become a favorite pass-time. It calms me and my wolf."

"I don't often have the opportunity to watch the sunset reflect against the sea. Black Thistle Castle isn't near the water. Of course, I have seen the colors of the night's sky before the stars chase them away, but it is much grander against the water."

"I often dream of living on a small island where I can see both the morning sunrise and the evening sunset against the water. My cottage would be set against a forest where my wolf could run without fear of being seen or captured. It is only a dream, but a beautiful dream nonetheless."

"Would you ever consider returning to Fallon Castle?"

"I could never go back to Fallon Castle. It would not be allowed."

"Surely your father's people would have had a change of heart by now."

"I would not be so bold as to bang my fist against the tall gate to ask for permission to enter. With the passing of my mother and father, I am sure their daughter has long been forgotten. They would only remember the wolf and turn me away."

"Black Thistle would never turn you away. Our gate is always open."

"Open to everyone?"

"It is open to almost everyone."

It is open to everyone but Velsa, he thought.

"Look, the sky is turning orange," she said. "We almost missed it."

They sat silently looking at the sky's bright orange slowly turn to a deep red and the clouds turn dark as the light from the sun began to fade. Feeling the sun had betrayed them both by setting so quickly, they made plans to watch it again.

"Best I get you back to your cottage."

He took her outstretched hand and pulled her to her feet. As she clutched her shawl, Gautier bushed the stray wisps of hair from her face. Cautiously he leaned down and lightly touched her lips with his own. When he drew back, she stood with her eyes closed and a warm blush upon her cheeks.

"May I have another, please?" she softly whispered.

"You may have as many as you desire, my sweet."

Gautier gently embraced her shoulders and pulled her close. Leaning down, he pressed his lips firmly against hers. As he did, he felt her wrap her arms around his waist and the pressure of her hands upon his back. Feeling her body start to tremble, he broke the kiss and slowly pulled back. Lifting her chin with his finger, he saw a single tear slip from her eye.

"Why the tears, my sweet?"

"It was my first kiss," she blushed. "Gautier, it was more wonderful than I could've ever imagined."

He pulled her close, and she rested her head against his chest.

"It was wonderful, my sweet. It was wonderful."

* * *

The first thing Gautier saw when he returned to the tavern was Lorcan tethering his horse to a wooden post. He knew what it meant, and he wasn't happy. He was being called back to Black Thistle.

"Lorcan, who has sent you to Woods Village?" Gautier shouted, as he approached his friend.

"My Lord, I have been sent by your brother to bring you home. There have been fires in the forest near the castle," replied Lorcan.

"My brother needs me to put out fires?"

"They are not ordinary fires. The flames glow with heat but do not burn the ground beneath them. It has caused the deer to scatter from the forest."

"What does Derora make of it?"

"She found magic surrounding the fires and the essence of dark magic. Derora has been unable to put out the fires. She believes the fires were created by Velsa, and she is dabbling in black magic."

"This is because of me. She is doing this because I let her go. What must I do to end this nonsense?"

"Your brother wants you to confront her and make her stop. He feels you are the only one that can. If you are unable, a warrant for her arrest will be issued."

"It's too late to head back to the castle tonight. I'll see that you have a room in the tavern, and we will leave at first light."

Chapter 7

Velsa's days had seemed long and her nights even longer since leaving Black Thistle Castle. She missed her bedchamber, the music, the dancing, and she missed Gautier most of all. Still angry about her dismissal, she tried the best she could to keep her mind busy. Since Balgair's visit, she had taken to collecting herbs and hanging them to dry from the beams of her cottage. The aroma that filled her cottage awakened a desire to practice her magic, and she looked forward to Balgair's return.

One afternoon while putting her books and bottles in order, her book of spells fell from its pedestal and started vibrating upon her table. Before she could pick it up, the cover flew open, and the pages fluttered madly back and forth as if searching for something. All at once, the fluttering stopped, and the pages laid open to a page scrawled with black ink. A spell had magically appeared in her book. Afraid to touch the page with her bare hand, she cautiously leaned over it to read the writing.

Whispering wind
    Fans the fire
Look within
    For what you desire

Dare to draw near

Examine the flame

A view will reveal

Who is to blame

Curious as to the nature of its power, she recited the spell over and over in her mind. The words were simple enough but strange nonetheless. She believed it to be a vision spell, but what was the catalyst. Snapping her fingers, her candle was brought to flame. Taking a deep breath, she recited the spell and waited. Slowly a tiny flame appeared before her and then faded away.

"That was less than impressive," she muttered.

Pulling a few strands of her hair from her head, she laid them across the written spell and recited the words again. Nothing happened.

"A candle doesn't work and neither does my hair. Blood . . . does it need blood?"

She knew the danger of using blood in a spell, and its ties to black magic. If she used her blood as the catalyst, she would allow the darkness to taste her blood. At that moment, they would be tied forever, and there would be no return.

Velsa paced back and forth wringing her hands trying to decide what to do. Just the idea of using her blood made her skin crawl, but it was also a little exciting too. After all, she needed some excitement after the way Gautier had treated her.

Opening a black chest by the small gold clasp, she reached into the thick black fabric and withdrew a dagger encrusted with rubies. It had been a gift from Gautier after he had returned from his first sea voyage. Shaking her head to chase away her memories, she pulled the dagger from its sheath. Placing the tip of the dagger in the palm of her hand, she pierced her flesh. While the blood pooled in her palm she recited the spell. As soon as the last word was spoken, large flames appeared before her. Startled, she dropped the dagger and stepped back away from the flames. She could feel the heat, but it was only a vision and burned nothing around her. Her eyes were drawn to a blue haze in the center of the flame. Confused, she thought about the words of the spell.

"Who do I blame for the love I have lost?"

Slowly the haze cleared to reveal Gautier's face.

"Why has he let me go?"

Gautier's face disappeared and the haze returned. Frustrated, she swept the flames away with her hand. Needing to know more, she recited the words again. A new flame appeared before her.

"Who holds Gautier's heart?"

The haze cleared, and the face of a woman appeared. She was fair with long hair that hung in soft curls the color of pale flax.

"Who is this woman?"

The woman's face disappeared and the haze returned. Angered by what she had seen, she waved her arm, and the flames vanished. Feeling the sting of his betrayal, Velsa screamed as she cursed Gautier's name. Sparks flew from her fingertips and singed the herbs that hung above her head. She collapsed to the floor and covered her face with her hands refusing to cry. Feeling something rough against her face, she pulled her hands away to see warts and dark age spots covered the skin. Her nails had thickened and turned a brownish yellow.

"Who has done this to me?"

Flames appeared and a vision of herself surrounded by darkness stared back at her. Furious, she stood and waved the flames away.

"You have ruined me, Gautier. In return, I shall ruin everything you hold dear. I shall ruin everything you love. I shall ruin you, and you will know that I have done so," she screamed, as purple sparks filled her cottage.

* * *

As Gautier entered the Great Hall, he immediately saw Astra deep in conversation with his brother. She was a wisp of a young woman with the fairest skin and hair he had ever seen. Even though she was a powerful witch trained by her mother in white magic, her unique ability to see the future gave her a seat on Lord Heinrich's council. Try as he may, she had turned down Lord Heinrich's numerous requests to live at the castle. She preferred to live a quiet life in Primrose Pond. Most assumed the shy witch had taken the cottage far from the castle for solitude, but Gautier knew the real reason. It was her sister, Velsa, that kept her at bay. They were friendly toward one another, but Velsa's competitive nature caused numerous conflicts between the two of them. To satisfy her peace of mind, Astra kept her distance from the castle and her sister.

Looking up and seeing Gautier, Gerwig placed his hand on Astra's arm to interrupt her.

"Brother, please join us. We were just discussing the problem Velsa has caused," shouted Gerwig.

"I saw the strange fires in the forest. Thankfully, they seem to be fading," Gautier replied, as he politely reached for Astra's hand and covered it with his own. "It has been much too long since your last visit, Astra. I have missed you."

"And, I have missed you, Gautier."

"Lorcan told me that Derora discovered your sister had a hand in this. Are they a danger to anyone?"

"They are harmless and will all fade in time," offered Astra.

"Astra came to me unannounced with troubling information. Not only has she seen the fires in the forest, but she has seen Velsa dabbling in black magic," grumbled Gerwig.

Gautier looked at Astra waiting for her to explain what she had seen. He could see the dread in her eyes.

"I can tell you only what I have seen," she explained. "Velsa has made a blood offering to the darkness, and there is no way to break this tie between them. Those fires in the forest are from a vision spell. As a novice in black magic, she has been discarding them not knowing how to dispose of them. As a result, they linger in the forest for anyone to see. If you look within the flames you will see what she has seen and know what she has learned."

"Have you seen what she has seen?" asked Gerwig.

Astra looked from Gerwig to his brother's worried face.

"Yes, I have seen Gautier's image and also that of the woman he calls Kayleigh. She is trying to find the woman she believes to be the reason he let her go."

"What woman is this?" asked Gerwig.

"I met a woman in Woods Village before you called me back to retrieve Lady Petula. It was an unexpected encounter. She stepped from a door and accidentally fell into my grasp. At that moment, I felt a rush of warmth up my arms. It proves she is my destiny," replied Gautier. "I was with her before you sent Lorcan to bring me back here."

"I heard her vow to ruin everything you hold dear," sighed Astra.

"If Velsa is hunting for Kayleigh, she is in danger. This is all my fault. I should have ended what Velsa and I shared a long time ago."

"Gautier, she has always been a little troubled. It isn't your fault. The darkness took advantage of her weakness," Astra replied.

"If your lady is in danger, bring her to Black Thistle. Between you and Derora, we should be able to protect her," ordered Gerwig.

"There is something else I must tell you. Kayleigh was banished from Fallon Castle by her father."

"Why would her father banish her?"

Gautier hesitated before he replied. "She was bitten by a wolf. He feared harm would come to his people, and he made her leave to survive on her own."

"I understand the desire to keep his people safe, but I could never turn away my own child," sighed Gerwig.

"Kayleigh managed to survive by keeping her wolf a secret. I discovered it and confronted her with it," Gautier rubbed his hand over his face in frustration. "Now, I have broken my promise to keep her secret safe. She will think I have betrayed her."

"She will understand if you explain it to her," Gerwig said, as he grasped his brother's shoulder. "Bring her here. She will be safe here. There is no one here at Black Thistle that will find her unworthy of our protection."

"Thank you, brother," he replied. "After I tell her what I have done, I hope she will be willing to accept your invitation."

"As do I. Now, go retrieve your mate and take Lorcan with you," ordered Gerwig.

Gautier placed his fist over his heart and bent down on one knee before his brother.

"My Lord, you honor me with this act of kindness."

* * *

When they finally arrived at Kayleigh's cottage, the sky was full of stars surrounding a full moon. It hadn't occurred to Gautier that her wolf could be within the forest until he heard a wolf's howl.

"Lorcan, go stand guard at her door. I'll wait here for her wolf to return."

As he watched Lorcan make his way to her cottage, he turned toward the forest and sat down to wait for her.

It wasn't long before he heard the sound of an animal running. With the help of the moonlight, he saw a glimpse of her beautiful wolf through the tall grass, and then she was gone.

Gautier snapped to his feet searching for her. There was no sign of her, anywhere. Fearing she had succumbed to a hunter's arrow, he ran toward the spot where he had last seen her. His hands brushed back and forth through the tall grass as he frantically searched for her.

Where are you, Kayleigh? Where are you?

With her nowhere in sight, he stood bewildered over where she could have gone. Hearing a slight rustling sound, he looked down to find Kayleigh's wolf standing beside him.

"You are safe," he cried, as he knelt down and was greeted by her wet tongue licking his neck and face.

He ran his fingers over her back and through her fur. Again, the warmth between them surged through his body. Feeling some trepidation, he pushed her head back and looked into her eyes.

"My little wolf, I am so glad to see you. Let's get you back to the cottage, we need to talk."

Gautier followed her through the tall grass toward a cluster of boulders. As she ducked her head, he saw what he thought was an entrance to a cave. Lifting her head, she looked back at him and then toward her cottage.

"Do you want me to go?"

She looked again in the direction of the cottage and quickly disappeared into the darkness. Gautier stood for a moment before he ran to meet Lorcan.

It wasn't long before Kayleigh opened the door and stepped out onto the porch to greet Gautier. Seeing Lorcan, she immediately stilled, and Gautier could see the fear in her eyes.

"This is Lorcan. He means you no harm."

"I am at your service, My Lady."

Concern filled Kayleigh's face, and Gautier quickly wrapped his arms around her.

"He is here for your protection."

Kayleigh pushed out of Gautier's arms and glared at him.

"Why would I need protection?"

"I have learned some things that I need to tell you. May I come in?"

She looked again at Lorcan and saw the boar and thistle markings on his chest. His attire made it clear, he was a member of the army. If the army was at her door, there was danger near. Still unnerved by his appearance, she was relieved he wasn't from Fallon Castle and nodded her head in agreement.

After Kayleigh was seated, Gautier took the chair next to her. He tried to take her hands, but she moved them away from his reach. Taking a deep breath, he leaned his arms against his thighs and clasped his hands as he looked at the floor.

"Before I tell you why I am here, I need to tell you that I have betrayed your trust. I have told my brother, Lord Heinrich, a member of his council, and Lorcan of the reason you were banished by your father."

Kayleigh sat quietly, but out of the corner of his eye, he could see her hands trembling in her lap.

"Lorcan was sent by my brother to bring me back to Black Thistle. When I arrived, I found my brother deep in conversation with Astra, a member of his council, a white witch, and the sister of Velsa."

Keeping his eyes toward the floor, he could see Kayleigh stand and move toward the hearth. His heart ached as she began pacing back and forth wringing her hands.

"As you know, I ended what was between Velsa and myself. Apparently, it has been met with great difficulty. I have been told that Velsa has been dabbling in black magic. She has been conjuring visions of me and of a woman she feels has replaced her." He heard Kayleigh gasp but knew he needed to continue. "In all the time I have known Velsa, I have never known her to hurt anyone; however, I won't take a chance with your safety. I want you to come back with me to Black Thistle Castle. There, I can protect you."

He looked up to see tears running down Kayleigh's face. As he stood, she turned away from him.

"Please go away," she sobbed. "If you go, there will be no reason for her to harm either of us."

"I can't leave without you."

"You must go, for I will not go with you. This is my home."

"You can make a new home in Black Thistle with me. Please, come back with me."

"Gautier, please leave. We are over. Tell Velsa it is done."

* * *

Velsa stood in the forest waving her arms in the air. Surrounded by blue smoke, she had no idea where it had come from or how to get rid of it. She had simply vanished from her cottage and appeared in the forest to be consumed by a strange blue substance.

It will certainly be difficult to sneak up on someone with this following me!

Seeing the last of the smoke gradually disappear, she stepped out from behind the trees and walked toward the cottage. A tendril of smoke swirled from the chimney, and she could smell something sweet in the air. Pushing her grey braid over her shoulder, she made her way to the door. Raising her hand to knock, she stopped and looked at the age spots that had discolored her creamy skin. Angered by the sight of them, she banged on the door with her fist. As the door opened, she was greeted by her sister's apprehensive smile.

"What brings you to Primrose Pond, Velsa?" Astra asked, as she took in Velsa's changed appearance. "Or, what I should ask is what brings you to my door?"

"Oh sister, we both know the reason for my visit. I am here to warn you to stay away from Gautier. I know that you have told him of my visions, and the woman he calls Kayleigh. I have seen in them both."

"Had he looked closely, he would have seen your visions himself. They were spread carelessly throughout the forest. Anyone could have seen them."

"If anyone could have seen them, why did you run to Lord Heinrich?"

"It was not only the visions that concerned me; it was the magic that was used to create them. I know you have let the darkness seep into your blood."

"You are correct, little sister. I have taken some of the darkness into my blood, and I will use it to retrieve what belongs to me."

"Will it be worth having, if his love is not returned?"

"It will return," she sneered and pointed her finger at Astra. "I will make it return."

"Velsa, his heart will be empty if you do this to him."

"I will do as I please. Stay away from Black Thistle Castle and Gautier. I am warning you, Astra! If you don't, I will send you far away from everyone and everything that is precious to you."

With that, Velsa vanished leaving a swirling wisp of blue smoke.

* * *

The sun was just beginning to set as Velsa walked through the square of Woods Village. The vendors were wheeling their carts away, and the ship's workmen were beginning to wander in from the bay. Music could be heard coming from the tavern, and the smell of rabbit stew filled the air. Her stomach grumbled from the day's neglect, and she made her way to the tavern's door.

Inside, she inhaled the tantalizing aroma as she searched for an empty table.

"Are you looking for an empty knee to sit upon?" a heavy man with an eyepatch shouted. "I have one for you."

"There is barely enough room on your knee for that belly that hangs upon it," yelled another man. "Where would she sit?"

Velsa scowled at the men and found her way to a small table in the corner. She watched a woman carrying two large steaming bowls toward a table next to her. After placing them down, the woman wiped her hands on her apron and looked over at Velsa.

"What can I get for you? You want ale or stew?"

"I'll be needing both."

A sudden cheer roared as a dagger pierced the center of a target painted on the far wall. As the man pulled his dagger from the target, he looked over his shoulder and caught sight of her looking at him. She noticed his smirk as he bent down to stow his dagger in his boot, and felt her heart begin to race. As he left the rowdy game, she watched him roll up the sleeves to his tunic all the while staring back at her. Before she knew it, he stood before her.

"Are you in need of some company?" he asked, as he pulled the empty stool out and sat down. He rested his arms on the table, one arm over the other, and stared into her eyes. "You look to be a bit lonely tonight."

She could feel her face flush, and the heel of her boot began to bounce uncontrollably against the floor. Try as she may, she couldn't pull her eyes away from his. As he raised his hand and touched her face, she heard herself whimper.

"My name is Tremayne . . . can you speak woman?"

Velsa blinked her eyes and felt dizzy.

"I am terribly sorry. I don't know what has come over me. My name is Velsa."

"You be wanting a little fun tonight?"

"What kind of fun are you offering?"

"A romp or two . . . more if you find it makes you merry."

Her bowl of stew and cup of ale arrived with a thud.

"That will be three coins," blurted Opal.

Velsa lifted her skirt and pulled three coins from her pouch that was tied above her knee. Holding out her hand, Opal scraped them from her palm and dropped them into her pocket, leaving as quietly as she had arrived.

"I'll be letting you eat your supper. If I'm still free once you've had your fill, I'll take you to my room."

Tremayne stood and leaned over placing both hands on the table. The sleeves of his tunic were rolled up exposing a tattoo of a winged ship just below his elbow and one of flames circling his wrist. The flames seemed to move, and she gently touched them with her fingers. Feeling the heat, she quickly pulled her hand away.

"Have a good meal, little witch," he whispered. "I'll be waiting."

* * *

Drifting down the tavern stairs, Velsa couldn't get Tremayne out of her mind. He had guided her upstairs to his room after her meal, and taught her things she never believed possible. When the morning sun had brightened the room, she had found herself alone. He had risen in the early morning hours to prepare to set sail by late afternoon. On his pillow he had left his metal cuff engraved with the sun he had worn about his wrist. Not knowing what to do with it, she clasped it around her ankle. After dressing, she had lifted her skirt numerous times to admire the memento. It would be a constant reminder of an encounter she would always remember.

Walking among the tavern tables, she saw the flurry of people outside, and she remembered the purpose of her visit.

"Madame Opal, can you help me?"

"What can I do for you?" Opal asked.

"I am looking for a young woman. She is fair in face and hair. I believe her to live here in Woods Village and go by the name Kayleigh. I was asked to pass along a message from her sister. Might you be able to help me?"

"You must mean Kay White. Madame White lives beyond the trees. Her cottage sits alone and faces the sea. It is a small cottage with a wooden porch. The path lined with wildflowers will take you directly there."

"Thank you for your help," she replied, as she touched her left shoulder with her index finger and tapped it three times. "You shall not remember me. Now, go to your kitchen and stir your boiling pot." Opal blinked her eyes several times before she turned and silently headed for the kitchen. "That was easy enough."

With the information she needed, Velsa left the tavern and headed for the path that would take her to the cliffs. It wasn't long before she saw the small weathered cottage. Determined to put the woman in her place, Velsa stepped up onto the wooden porch and approached the door. Closing her eyes, she envisioned Kayleigh's face and what she wanted to say to her. Before she could rap on the door, the door opened and Kayleigh stood before her. Velsa was stunned by the woman's beauty. Trying to speak, she choked on her words until they finally sprang free.

"My name is Velsa."

She could see what she thought was fear in Kayleigh's eyes.

"I am not here to hurt you, but I am here to offer a warning. Stay away from Gautier. You see, he has always belonged to me. If you don't; however, you will pay dearly. I am not known for giving second chances and can easily harm everyone you hold dear. Do you understand?"

Kayleigh nodded as she watched Velsa vanish. Blue smoke swirled in her place as she closed the door. Leaning her head against the door, she began to cry.

"I can't stay here anymore. I have to leave this place to protect Gautier."

She gathered the few belongings she would need and stowed them in a bag she had made from rabbit pelts. Tearing a piece of parchment from her journal, she dipped the tip of her quill in her bottle of ink and began to write.

My dearest Gautier,

Your Velsa came to my door.

She stood before me, and her warnings were clear.

I must leave this place and my heart behind.

For it will always belong to you.

Always and forever, Your Kayleigh

Leaving the note on the small table, she hoped that Gautier would find it. Kayleigh reached for the handle of the door. Looking back one last time, she opened it and ran for the harbor.

Chapter 8

After asking everyone on the dock, Kayleigh discovered there was only one ship, the Christaline's Slipper, that was ready to depart the island, and there wouldn't be another ship ready to sail for six days. Left with no other options, the ship sailing to the Isle of Tears was her only choice to escape the threats made by Velsa. She knew nothing of this island, but the name conjured nothing but sadness. It would be the perfect place for her to live out her days, if she was strong enough to keep living with a broken heart.

The voyage was long, and the dreadful rocking motion kept her constantly nauseous. It was all she could do to drag herself up to the main deck once a day for fresh air and to empty her bucket. She found rest whenever she could, for her bunkmate entertained the ship's crew in the evening offering her an endless serenade of grunting and moaning.

By mid-afternoon on the fourth day of the voyage, the fog finally lifted and the sunshine burst through the clouds. Closing her eyes, she lingered in its warmth until she heard the sound of exuberant shouting and cheering that brought her running to the port side of the ship. Far off in the distance, she could see a thin strip of land, and her mind was filled with a sense of relief that she would soon set foot on dry land. Eager for a glimpse of the island, she stood leaning against the railing watching the thin strip of land grow larger and larger. It wasn't until she could see the trees of the forest that she could feel her anxious wolf sigh.

Upon their arrival, the crack of the gangplank hitting the dock sent shivers up her spine. She was suddenly filled with emotions she hadn't felt since the day her father banished her from her home. With her bag over her shoulder, she walked toward what she hoped would be a good life for her and her wolf.

* * *

Gautier had kept his distance hoping that Kayleigh would change her mind after thinking about what he had told her, but he couldn't wait any longer. He had to see her and hold her in his arms again. Unable to deal with the thought of her being alone, he sent Lorcan back to the castle, and he raced for Woods Village.

As he approached her cottage door, an eerie sense of dread caused him to halt. He listened for the sound of the fire in her hearth or her footsteps against the wooden floor. Hearing nothing, he slowly opened the door and called her name. The room was cold and the usual bright hearth was empty. As a cool breeze whipped over his shoulder, he saw something flutter to the floor. Picking it up, he stood dazed as he read her note. Crumbling it in his hand, a vile taste filled his mouth as he spit out Velsa's name.

Closing her cottage door, he searched his mind for a place that she would hide.

Would she return to Wintergreen Mountain or beg for shelter at Fallon Castle? With Velsa's command of visions, she could easily locate Kayleigh anywhere on the island. She would have to leave to protect herself.

Mounting his horse, Gautier raced to the harbor. He knew that boarding a ship would be her only chance to hide herself from Velsa's clutches. Arriving at the dock, he grabbed the first man within his reach.

"Have there been any ships set sail in the past two days?" asked Gautier.

"Only one was Christaline's Slipper," replied the man.

"Where was it bound?"

"It set sail for the Isle of Tears."

"When will another head that way?"

"Not until she returns in eight days and loads its cargo."

Gautier released the man's arm and hunched over grabbing his knees. Pain cut into his chest as he tried to breathe. It would be two weeks before he could reach the Isle of Tears and search for her. She would be alone in a place completely foreign to her, and it was all his fault.

Knowing there was nothing he could do until then, he reluctantly mounted his horse. Returning to Black Thistle without her would be painful, but he would take the time to counter Velsa's intrusions. He would conjure his own spell to block Velsa from finding him or his beautiful Kayleigh.

* * *

Velsa sat with her legs propped up on her milking stool and her skirt pulled up to her knees while she admired the metal cuff around her ankle. She had not removed it since finding it on the pillow beside her. The memories of her one night spent in the arms of Tremayne had kept her face flushed for days. That and the look of fear upon Kayleigh's pale face had made her visit to Woods Village one she would always remember.

Feeling tired for absolutely no reason, she leaned her head back against her chair to rest. She had just closed her eyes when her cottage door began to vibrate. Startled by the strange humming sound that grew to a painful roar, she hurried to the door and yanked it open. Holding her hands over her ears, she could see the wind swirling in front of her doorway and felt it attempting to draw her out of her cottage. Reaching for the frame of the door, she struggled to hold herself back from its strange power. As her feet lifted up into the air, she felt her fingernails snap as she was pulled outside, and the wind encircled her body. Confused, she franticly tried to escape, but it quickly replied with a tighter grasp. Suspended up in the air, the sting of whispered words whirled about her head. As the whispers grew louder, blood began to run from her ears and the sunlight suddenly vanished. There in the dark, she felt a thick haze crawl against her skin and enter the pores of her body. As quickly as it had started, the wind calmed, and Velsa dropped to the ground.

Afraid to open her eyes, she felt the warmth of the sun upon her face before she opened one eye and then the other.

What in the world was that?

Velsa sat for a moment trying to make sense of what happened. The sound of the wind was nothing new to her. It often brought her messages or allowed her to eavesdrop, but the messages were never delivered so violently.

It was as if someone had cursed me, she thought.

Slowly it dawned on her what had happened. A spell had been cast, and she had been the recipient. Her hands began to tremble and small sparks flew from her fingertips. As she struggled to stand, she carelessly tripped on the hem of her skirt. Once secure on her feet she brushed the dirt from her scrapped hands and silently cursed the ground for her wounds. After picking several twigs from her hair and wiping dirt from her face with the back of her hand, Velsa gave up and headed for the safety of her cottage.

Back inside, Velsa paced back and forth across the length of her tiny cottage. Someone had cast a spell upon her, and she was determined to find out who sent it. Even more, she needed to know its meaning and how to counteract it. With both hands pressed down upon the top of her table, she recited the words to call the vision spell forward, and its flame immediately appeared before her.

"Who has cast this curse upon me?"

The center of the flame revealed the image of a person behind a dark cloudy fog. The image was too dark to reveal anything useful in determining if it was a man or a woman. Unsatisfied and needing an answer, she swept the vision away with her hand and recited the words again. As the flame appeared, she pondered her next question.

"What is the curse's purpose?

The center of the flame turned black.

"Vision, you show me nothing," screamed Velsa. Turning her back on the useless vision, she raked her teeth over her bottom lip. "It shows me nothing. What good are you? It shows me nothing. It shows me nothing." Turning around, she stared at the dark center of the flame and tried to consider its meaning. Suddenly, it became clear to her. "Why didn't I see it? That is the purpose . . . to show me nothing." Pleased with herself, she flipped her braid over her shoulder and laughed. "It is blocking me. It is a protection spell."

Flicking the vision away, Velsa's laughter filled her cottage. She knew the only people needing protection from her were Gautier and Kayleigh. Knowing that, it was easy to surmise that Gautier had been the one to cast the spell. He was certainly strong enough to counter any of her spells. If he wanted to play games, she would be happy to play along, but for now, she would wait for just the right moment. After all, she could afford to wait. She would always win with the darkness by her side.

* * *

Gautier had painstakingly created a spell to hide himself and Kayleigh from Velsa's prying eyes. The day it had been cast and sent searching for her wicked heart, he felt its fearless attack and her desperate struggle against it. He had deliberately sent it with the wind to weaken her defenses, allowing the haze time to seep into every pore of her body. With Velsa's vision blocked, he was now free to sail to the Isle of Tears to search for Kayleigh.

* * *

Kayleigh jumped from the back of the wagon and waved to the elderly man that had graciously offered her a ride from the dock to the small village of Moss Rock. As she looked around, she noticed several buildings carefully fashioned from stones of unequal size covered with roofs of neatly tied thatching. Knowing darkness would soon be upon her, she searched for the village tavern in hopes of finding a room for the night in exchange for some domestic chores. Hearing a strange creaking sound behind her, she was pleased to find it came from the sign above the Moss Rock Tavern.

Taking a deep breath, she pushed open the door and looked about for the owner. The room was empty except for a small table surrounded by men tossing small bones from a wooden cup. Bewildered by what they were doing, she stood and watched until she felt someone tap her on the shoulder.

"They are playing Knucklebones," the woman laughed. "The bones in the cup are from a sheep's ankle. Each side of the bone is different and each side of the bone is worth different points. They throw the bones on the table and count the points. The winner has the most points."

"It looks fun," replied Kayleigh, as she continued to watch the men play.

"Missy, what can I get for you?" the woman asked.

Pulled away from watching the game, she looked directly at the woman.

"My name is Kayleigh, and I have just arrived today on the Christaline's Slipper. I need a room or a safe place to sleep for the night. I am willing to work for my bed. I can cook, clean, or anything you need done," replied Kayleigh. "I'm not afraid of hard work."

She could see that the woman was pondering her request, and she hoped the sight of her wouldn't cause her to be driven away. Four days at sea without a bath had put her in quite an undesirable state.

"I have some berries that need hulling and bread to make for tomorrow. If you can help me in the kitchen, I can give you the small room off the kitchen for the night."

"Thank you, Madame."

"You may call me Maw. I'm called that by most of the young ones around here, and you look as young as anyone that has passed through here lately." Shaking her head, Maw eyed the hem of Kayleigh's skirt and the soil on her apron. "Child, let's get you cleaned up. I'll take you to your room and bring you some fresh water."

Kayleigh was thrilled with the kindness Maw had shown her and eagerly followed her through the doorway to the kitchen. The small room she had been offered was indeed very small. It was deep enough for a cot and wide enough for the stool to fit snuggly between the cot and the wall.

"Will it do," asked Maw.

"It will do just fine," Kayleigh replied, as she placed her bag on the floor by the cot.

Seeing Maw put a kettle on the fire, she began removing her clothes. Standing in nothing but her under-slip, she wrapped her arms around herself as she remembered the copper tub in her bathing room at Fallon Castle. It was a luxury she hadn't thought about for years and would never see again.

"Here you go, child," Maw said, as she handed her a small piece of soap and placed a folded piece of linen on the cot. "When you are finished, I'll help you rinse your hair. I have another kettle of water ready for you."

She watched Maw place the bucket of hot water on the stool and pick up her dirty clothes from the floor.

"Don't mind the floor, the water will be good for it. I'll mop it when you're done."

Completely taken by the kindly old woman, Kayleigh picked up the soap and thrust her hands into the water to make a lather. As she scrubbed the dirt from her body, she inhaled the fresh clean scent of the soap. It reminded her of the lavender and sage that grew around the Old Stone Tower in Woods Village. After untangling her braid, she dunked her hair into the bucket and lathered it the best she could. Squeezing out as much water as she could, she saw Maw snatch the bucket and toss the dirty water out the open door.

"Come stand on the bucket. You won't get your feet muddy," Maw beckoned. "Don't be shy. No one will see you."

Kayleigh scurried out the door and stood with both feet on the bottom of the upside down bucket.

"Now, bend over and I'll rinse the soap from your hair."

As Maw poured the water, Kayleigh moved her hands through her hair to help remove the soap. Once the water ran clear, she twisted the strands of her hair to remove as much water as she could and tucked it into a knot.

"Get inside before you catch a chill. Put on your sleeping gown and come sit by the fire to dry your hair."

Kayleigh was overwhelmed with Maw's kindness. Had she been sent away, she would have been forced to shift into her wolf to keep from shivering out in the cold night air. She would have also missed the pleasure of sweet smelling soap dunked in warm water to wash her face.

With her hair dry from the heat of the fire and dressed in clean clothes, she stood at Maw's table with two large pails of berries before her. As she listened to Maw hum a tune, she worked away at hulling the wild strawberries. Trying to keep thoughts of Gautier out of her head, she thought about what she had seen of the island. She was more than curious about how it had gotten its name.

"Maw?" asked Kayleigh.

"Yes child," Maw replied.

"This island is called the Isle of Tears. It sounds so sad. How did it get its name?"

"My child, the mountains get rain almost every day, and it creates the most beautiful waterfalls all over the island. Legend has it that fairies once lived on this island. They took care of the wildflowers that are scattered from Moss Rock all the way up to Watcher's Point. They did it for the bees and for themselves. You see, the bees' sweet nectar was the source of the fairies' magic. One day a disgruntled troll poisoned the sweet nectar. One by one the fairies got sick and died."

"That story makes me want to cry. Is that why they call it the Isle of Tears?"

"No, there is more to the tale. The fairies' spirits rose to the stars. They missed their flowers so much; they begged Mother Earth to plant wildflowers in the clouds. She happily agreed to their request, and the fairies were overjoyed. So, it is a happy tale after all. When you see the rain, you will know that it is the fairies' tears of happiness that spill from the clouds as they water their flowers. Their tears create the waterfalls. Thus, the island was named Isle of Tears."

"I love this story. Why is it kept a secret? Just hearing the Isle of Tears makes me think that terrible things happen here."

"I suppose it keeps people from coming here. We lead a quiet life. You will find the people here are friendly, and we take pride in helping one another."

"Maw, I am so thankful for the help you have provided me, but I need to find a place to live. I can't stay in your kitchen forever. Do you know where I might find a small cottage."

"There is a small stone cottage just beyond Duck's Puddle. No one has lived there since Old Man Archer passed on. It is probably a dreadful sight inside. There hasn't been anyone seeking to claim it. So, I believe you have a new home. After the morning meals have been served, I will show you the way, and we'll see what must be done to make it livable."

"I am so relieved. I can't wait to see it."

***

With the morning meals served and the kitchen cleaned, Kayleigh and Maw left the tavern to make the long walk to Old Man Archer's cottage.

"Are you ready to see your new home?" asked Maw.

"Ready and eager to make it my own," replied Kayleigh. "A roof over my head and a fire in my hearth will be all the comfort I need."

"Let's hope it has a roof," laughed Maw.

The women talked and laughed as they proceeded up the well-worn path toward the mountains until Maw's curiosity could not be contained any longer.

"I've been wondering what has brought you to the island?" Maw asked.

"It is a long story," Kayleigh replied.

"We have a long walk ahead of us, and I am willing to listen."

Kayleigh could feel knots in her stomach as she tried to put her thoughts in order. Taking a deep breath, she decided to offer Maw the truths that she was willing to tell. If she mentioned anything about Velsa's warnings or that she was a wolf, she was sure to find herself run from the village, or worse yet, they would make her leave the island.

"One day, I literally fell into a man's arms as I left our village market. When I looked up to see who had saved me, his eyes stole my breath away. Embarrassed by the flush I could feel on my cheeks, I quickly left his side. Later, he discovered me walking to help Mr. Brumley and boldly set me upon his horse to save me the walk. After that meeting, it was some time before I saw him again. When he returned, he left an apple on my porch and brought me wildflowers. We talked and dined on rabbit stew. As we watched the sunset, he gave me my first kiss. Not long after that, I discovered that another woman was in love with him. I felt my heart break, and I could not bear the pain of it. So, I ran from the island." Kayleigh quickly wiped the tears away from her eyes. "And, here I am."

"You left him without saying good-bye?"

"I was a coward and left him a note."

"Well, I am willing to bet a plump chicken that your gentleman is searching for you right now, and he wants to set things right between the two of you. I can feel it in my bones, and my bones are never wrong."

Looking up, she gave Maw a half-hearted smile, "Me too."

A ruckus of quaking and splashing water made Kayleigh climb the small grassy berm to see where the noise was coming from. To her surprise, a dozen ducks paddled about the surface of a very large pond. Starting to laugh, she looked back at Maw.

"This is Duck's Puddle? I was expecting a puddle not a pond."

"Indeed it is, and a lovely puddle too." Seeing Maw struggling to climb the small berm, Kayleigh offered Maw her hand and pulled her up to allow her to stand beside her. "See the cottage over there by the trees? That is Old Man Archer's cottage."

The tall grass that surrounded the cottage nearly hid it from view. If it had not been pointed out to her, she never would have seen it. Shielding her eyes from the sun, she tried to take stock of its condition.

"Best we keep walking. We'll need the light to see what gifts the old man has left behind."

Standing as close as she could get to the door, Kayleigh began pulling the tall grass and weeds that impeded her path. With Maw's help, they soon had a narrow path cleared to the wooden door. Pushing with both hands, the door moved only a small amount. Taking a deep breath, she put her shoulder to the door and leaned as hard as she could. Feeling it move a little, Maw helped her force the door open.

The stench immediately caused Kayleigh to cover her nose and mouth with both hands. Thinking it was some dead animal, she quickly realized it was only mold and not the smell of death. It could be easily scrubbed away and the smell with it.

Slowly, light filled the room as Maw began opening the shuttered windows. With the sunlight spilling around the room, the stone hearth with its black cooking pot was the first thing Kayleigh spotted. To the left of the hearth tucked in the corner was a small table, a bench tipped on its side, and a large pail.

As Maw pulled the tattered mattress the rest of the way off the bed frame, feathers and rat droppings fell to the floor. Disgusted, she dropped it.

"You've been left a bed, but the ropes will need to be restrung," choked Maw, as she waved the feathers from her face. "Now, to find the straining wrench?"

Moving the small bed aside, Maw found the wrench on the floor near the head of the bed. As she waved it in the air, she noticed the frown upon Kayleigh's face.

"This isn't much to start with," sighed Kayleigh. "I only brought the few things I could carry in my bag."

"Not to worry, the people in the village will come to your aide. Until your cottage is livable, you can stay in your room at the tavern. I can use the help in the kitchen."

"You've done so much already; I don't know how to thank you."

"There is time enough for thanking. Let's get back to the tavern. Folks will be looking for their supper."

* * *

The days that followed found Maw's claim to be true. Every day after Kayleigh's morning chores at the tavern were complete, she made her way to her small stone cottage, and every day there were folks standing ready to help make her cottage livable.

The men had cleared all of the tall grass and weeds from the ground around the cottage, and a plot had been tilled to allow for the planting of a garden. Kayleigh had watched two men climb up onto the roof and repair the thatch where they had found it to be too thin. A small coup had been built from scraps of wood they had found in the tall grass, and wildflowers had been planted on either side of her door by two small children.

The women had helped her scrub the walls and the floor until the smell of mold was completely gone. The tattered mattress had been removed and replaced with one filled with fresh straw, and an elderly woman had even taught her how to tighten the ropes on the bed with the wrench.

After placing her blanket across the foot of her bed, she looked around at all of the odds and ends that filled her cottage. The people of Moss Rock had truly been generous with their time and their goods, and she vowed to repay them one day for their kindness.

* * *

Kayleigh had spent the afternoon searching for a path that would lead her wolf deep into the forest and far away from any danger. The path she had found was lined with small streams and thick with trees to keep her well protected. After choosing to find the source of the water that fed the streams, she had discovered a small meadow littered with wildflowers and surrounded by boulders covered in a thick layer of moss. Just beyond the meadow was the most beautiful waterfall she had ever seen. It fell from the mountain like a veil that gently spilled into a sapphire pool at the bottom. Watching the water crash against the rocks, she noticed something that appeared to be the remains of a stone wall. She had tried to get closer, but the water had kept her from going any further. Knowing it was getting late, she decided to return to her cottage and explore it another day.

She stood in her doorway looking at the sun as it prepared to give itself over to the first full moon since her arrival at Moss Rock. Her wolf was eager to run and had been begging to be released long before she had returned from the forest. Making sure that her cottage was dark, she closed the door and walked to the back of the cottage. Slowly, she removed her sleeping gown and folded it before placing it on the ground. As she crouched down in the sweet grass, she felt the excitement of her wolf before she burst forward and leapt for the cover of the forest.

The white wolf raced through the trees staying true to the path she had been shown. She inhaled the scents of the forest and longed for the challenge of the hunt. Stopping for only a moment to quench her thirst, she ran until she reached the meadow. Cautiously creeping out among the wildflowers, she laid down to rest.

The distant howl of a wolf woke her, and she searched for any sign of it. Fearing it may have discovered her, she ran for the cover of the forest and her cottage. After shifting back into her human form, Kayleigh quickly pulled her sleeping gown over her head and pulled it down to cover her naked body. As she turned to run for her door, she sensed a wolf before she heard a deep growl that sent ice-cold shivers up her back. Looking over her shoulder, she saw two golden eyes staring at her from the darkness of the trees. Fighting to keep her wolf hidden, she ran for the door. Opening it, she hurried inside and slammed the door. After putting the wooden brace in place to secure the door, she collapsed on the floor. Pulling her knees against her chest, she wrapped her arms tightly around her legs and listened as it circled her cottage.

The faint sound of barking dogs and men shouting jolted her to her feet. She could hear the wolf as it raced for the forest. It wasn't long before she heard fists pounding on her door.

"Mistress Kayleigh, are you safe? Have you been harmed?"

Recognizing Collin's voice, she removed the brace and opened the door enough to see him along with Sherman and his dogs standing at her door.

"The dogs caught the scent of a wolf, Mistress Kayleigh. Best you keep your door locked for the night," he said, as he held a lantern up toward her face. "We saw a black wolf run for the trees. Hopefully, it won't be back tonight."

"I'll keep my door locked. Thank you for scaring it away."

Collin and Sherman nodded and led the dogs away.

After securing her door, Kayleigh crawled into bed and pulled her blanket up under her chin. Closing her eyes, she tried to force the image of the wolf's golden eyes from her mind. Giving up, she tried to remember the scent that lingered in the air as she opened the door to Collin. It had been faint, but it smelled of musk and smoke. She knew she would recognize the scent if she came across it again.

* * *

The next morning, the tavern buzzed with the talk of Collin and Sherman chasing a wolf from her cottage door. She could hear Collin bragging about making the black wolf run for the safety of the forest and holding back his dogs from the chase. Sherman repeatedly tried to declare his own bravery, but Collin insisted he had been the one to put the fear in the beast.

As Collin's boasting quieted, Kayleigh placed plates of bread laden with cheese and bowls of porridge covered in berries on their tables. While walking among the tables, she listened to the men discussing a plan to hunt down the black wolf. Each man had an opinion on how best to take down the wolf, and every other man explained why his plan was no better than his own. Before long, shouting and fists pounding the tables drew Maw's attention, and she stormed into the room.

"If you don't quiet down, I'll be using this broom handle on each and every one of your heads," she shouted, as she banged the handle of her broom on the floor.

Clearly, she had their attention, for the rest of their meal was eaten in silence before they headed for the tavern door. With them gone, Kayleigh carried the empty plates, bowls, and mugs off to the kitchen.

"Did the wolf frighten you last night?" asked Maw.

"I knew there was something circling my cottage. I didn't know it was a wolf until Collin and Sherman knocked on my door to warn me," replied Kayleigh. "Are their many wolves on the island?"

"Many years ago, a black wolf was spotted near Watcher's Point by some men while they were hunting. It followed them, but kept a safe distance between them. The men assumed he was waiting to grab their kill for his own. After a while, the wolf gave up and vanished into the trees. No one has seen another wolf until last night at your cottage."

"Yesterday, I went for a walk in the forest. I came across a waterfall that spilled into a sapphire pool. Maybe it was there watching me."

"I would stay out of the forest until the men can find the wolf and put it down. You would be defenseless against a wild animal."

"I hope they find it soon. I want to go back to the waterfall. I saw some peculiar stones behind the water. Do you know what they might be?"

"I have heard others speak of a tunnel behind the falls that takes you to what is left of an old castle on the other side of the mountain. Several stories have been told of the old castle. The one I heard as a child was my favorite."

"Please, tell me."

"In the castle lived Lord and Lady Belmont. They had a beautiful daughter that used to walk in the shallow curling water of the sea. One day, a pirate ship anchored not far from the rocks beneath the castle. It was said that the Captain of the ship had spied the young woman and wanted her for his bride. He and a few of his men approached her father to ask for her hand. Her father refused and sent them away. That night while everyone was sleeping, the Captain kidnapped the young woman from the castle. In the morning, it was discovered she was gone and so was the pirate ship. Lord and Lady Belmont began searching for their daughter. Sadly, they never found her. The castle is all that remains."

"The ending was so sad. I was hoping for a happy ending."

"Such is life, my child."

Kayleigh sighed as she thrust the plates into the hot water. She had longed for her parents to have a change of heart and search for her. Now, it was too late. They were gone, and she was determined to make a good life without them.

Chapter 9

Gautier heard the smack of the gangplank as it hit the dock. The Christaline's Slipper had finally arrived at the Isle of Tears. With his sack over his shoulder, he strode down the wooden plank to begin the search for his beloved Kayleigh. Several wagons were lined up ready to be loaded, and he bothered one driver for directions to the tavern. Even though he had been offered a ride into Moss Rock, he decided to walk. It would give him time to think about what he would say to her.

The sun was high in the sky, and his brow was quite damp by the time he reached the tavern. As he opened the door, he recognized the smell of duck pie, and it made his mouth water. Looking around, he saw the tavern was empty and hoped that meant there would also be an empty room.

"Can I help you?" Maw shouted, from the kitchen doorway.

"I'll be needing a room for the night and a meal to warm my belly. I must say, the fine smell of your cooking has my mouth watering."

Maw had heard sweet talk before from those that wanted something for nothing, and she wanted to make it clear that she expected coin for her labor.

"It will be four coins for your room with two meals a day. A bath will cost you one more. If that meets with your approval, I'll show you to your room?"

"Lead the way, Madame."

Gautier followed Maw up the stairs and down the hallway to the last door on the right. The wooden floors creaked beneath his boots and made him think of the sound of Kayleigh's bare feet walking across the floor of her cottage.

"From the looks of your clothes, you might find this a bit plain, but it is clean."

"Don't be fooled by my clothes, Madame. I was taught to appreciate all that is offered to me and show respect to those that offer it. The room will be fine."

Maw smiled and opened the door for him to enter. Gautier sat his sack down and took in the simplicity of the furnishings. Taking a small pouch from his waist, he handed it to Maw.

"I may need to stay longer than one night. Let me know when you need more. I'll also be needing a horse."

Maw felt the weight of the pouch and quickly dropped it into the pocket of her apron.

"There is a small stable across the way. Make your bargain with Otis, not his son."

"Thanks for the warning."

Seeing the stubble on his face, she was curious about her new boarder.

"What brings you to Moss Rock?"

"I have come in search of someone very dear to me. A misunderstanding has separated us, and I have come to mend it."

She had heard a similar story from Kayleigh, and she was sure that this was the man that Kayleigh longed to see again. Maw smiled and gently rested her hand upon his arm.

"I believe I know the lady you are seeking. She has taken the cottage just beyond Duck's Puddle. Follow the dirt road until you see the pond. Her cottage sits against the trees. You can easily cross through the meadow to reach her door."

Gautier quickly bent down and kissed her cheek.

"You have set my heart to racing. You can't imagine how much I have missed her."

Feeling his excitement, she stepped from his room and rubbed the palms of her hands together.

"Now, let's get you fed. It is a long ride to Duck's Puddle."

* * *

After a quick conversation with Otis, the reins of a chestnut mare named Agatha were handed over in exchange for ten coins. Five of which would be returned to him when Agatha was returned to the stable. After mounting the mare, Otis slapped her hind quarters, and she slowly left the stable. Once they reached the center of the road, he heard Otis shout.

"Tie her to a post, or she will head for home the first chance she gets. You'll find it's a long walk back."

"Agatha, you have something in common with my Kayleigh. You both like to flee," whispered Gautier, as he stroked the black mane that draped along her neck.

The ride was slow, and the hot sun made it feel even slower. Finally reaching the pond, he dismounted and led sweet Agatha to the pond for a drink. Being certain to secure the reins beneath his boot, he dipped his hands into the pond and splashed the cool water against his face. With his hands still wet, he rubbed them across the back of his neck as he stood and searched for the cottage.

"There it is, Agatha. That is where my Kayleigh lives."

Throwing his leg over the mare's back, he gently nudged her with the heel of his boot, and they headed toward the cottage.

* * *

The knock at her door caught her completely off-guard. Not expecting anyone, she peered through the small window by the door and saw a horse tied to an old post. Thinking it might be the young lad Maw had promised would help her in her garden, she went to the door. As she placed her hand on the handle, she hesitated for a moment and quickly pulled her hand away.

Could it be the person that takes the form of the black wolf?

She searched the air for the scent of musk and smoke. Relieved by its absence, she opened the door. The low afternoon sun was shining directly in her eyes, and its brightness caused her to lower them to the ground. She found herself staring at a man's black boots. She had seen them before.

"You open the door to anyone?" scolded Gautier. "It could have been a thief from the ship anchored in the bay. Who knows what harm he could have caused you."

Kayleigh gasped and stepped back away from the door. As he moved to block the sun from her eyes, she looked up at the face she had envisioned every night before she closed her eyes. It had been the face she dreamt about, and the face she had longed to see again.

"I can't believe that you are here."

"You did make it difficult, but where else would I be, if not with you?"

"I dare not say her name. It has brought so much heartache and sadness to my life."

He could see the sadness in her eyes, and it pained him to know that Velsa had been the cause.

"Velsa and I were never bound to one another. It was something she desired of me, but I could never bring myself to fulfill her desires. Now, I know the reason. I had been waiting for you, Kayleigh. All this time, I had been waiting for you."

Kayleigh rushed toward Gautier, and she felt him wrap his strong arms around her.

"I hoped you would come for me," she whispered.

"I promise you; I will always come for you," he replied. "Always."

Picking her up, he stepped inside and kicked the door closed before setting her down. He brushed the stray wisps of hair from her face and gently kissed her forehead. Keeping his lips against her skin, he reveled in the way a single touch could set his body ablaze. The sound of Kayleigh's soft sigh was too much for him, and he claimed her mouth with his own. He felt the eagerness of her tongue begin to explore his own, and the soft caress of her hands upon his back. Fearing he would lose control, he released her and took a step back. Looking down at the flush upon her cheeks, he gently stroked the side of her face with the back of his hand.

"You are my life, Kayleigh. You are everything I want and all that I need. I want to take you back to Black Thistle Castle."

Hearing his request, she opened her eyes and covered his hand with her own.

"Please, it is too soon. Let's not talk of leaving. After all, you have just arrived. Let's spend our time together getting to know each other without the fear of retaliation from . . . her.

Gautier felt the pain of her rejection, but he wasn't willing to give up.

"If you are happy here, I will submit to your desires.

"I was happy, but I am happier now that you are here with me. Come, sit by the fire with me."

Gautier sat down on the floor in front of the hearth. As she knelt down to sit beside him, he pulled her into his lap. She leaned back against his chest, and he kissed the top of her head.

"Is your wolf happy here? Has she run with the moonlight?"

"She has run once, and it had a disastrous end."

"Disastrous, how? Was she hurt?"

"No, we heard the howl of another wolf, and it followed her through the forest. Once she returned to the cottage and gave herself over to me, I quickly slipped my gown over my head and headed for my door. That is when I saw the wolf's eyes staring at me from the darkness of the trees. After I was safely inside, it paced around the cottage until men from the village and their dogs chased it away. I remembered smelling the faint scent of musk and smoke when I opened the door. Gautier, I think it is a wolf shifter like me."

"Even if it is, there could still be danger. I will cast a protection spell around your cottage before I leave this evening. It will ward off any animals trying to enter your cottage."

"That will protect me here, but how do I find out who shifts into that wolf?"

"The scent you caught the night the wolf circled your cottage should give their presence away. If you notice it again, don't give your discovery away. If it knows that you have found them, they may cause you harm."

"How can I allow my wolf to run in the forest with that wolf roaming around?"

"I'll stay in the forest with you. If it sees me, it may sense my magic and stay away."

Kayleigh sensed the setting sun and could feel her wolf begging to be set free. One run in the forest had not nearly satisfied her yearning for the crisp night air, the earth beneath her paws, or the glow of the moonlight among the trees. Sitting up and turning to face Gautier, she raked her teeth against her bottom lip before she spoke.

"My wolf wants to run tonight. She is begging me to let her free. We won't be alone if you go with us. Will you go with us?"

Gautier could feel the excitement in her voice, and he nodded.

Kayleigh stood and walked toward her bed.

"Don't turn around, and don't be alarmed at what you hear."

Gautier sat quietly looking at the flames that danced in the hearth as she removed her clothing, but he jerked when he heard her muffled cry mingled with the sound of bones popping and cracking. It wasn't until the quiet had replaced her cries that he felt his shoulders relax.

"Kayleigh, do you need my help?"

He felt her reply as her wet nose nuzzled his neck, and her tongue licked the side of his face. Getting up on his knees, he turned to face her wolf. Her white fur glistened in the firelight as she moved toward him.

"I would be perfectly content to sit with you by the fire with my hands caressing your fur, but I understand it is a run that you long for."

Making his way to the door, he opened it and peered out to see the orange glow of the setting sun. Making sure that Agatha was still secure, he motioned for her wolf to follow him. Without hesitation, she bolted through the open doorway and raced for the forest. Agatha merely lifted her head for a moment and then dropped her head to continue nibbling the sweet grass beneath her feet.

The white wolf eagerly waited for Gautier to follow. As soon as she saw him, she turned and raced for the stream. She could hear him running behind her, and she slowed her pace to allow him to keep her in his sight. Remembering the waterfall and the sapphire pool, she followed the path she had previously taken, but took the time to scent the air for any signs of the black wolf.

Reaching the clearing, she ran to the water's edge and lowered her head for a cool drink. Hearing Gautier behind her, she turned to watch his reaction when he took in the breathtaking view she had found so fascinating.

He stood gazing up at the height of the waterfall before he said, "I have no words to describe the beauty of this place."

After making a game of chasing Gautier through the meadow, Kayleigh's wolf was ready to return to the cottage. Instead of racing off ahead of him, she walked slowly by his side until they reached the back of the cottage. There, she waited for the sound of Gautier opening her door. Hearing it, she raced for the safety of her cottage.

Gautier gazed out the window as Kayleigh shifted back into her human form. He was pleased they had returned, for he had noticed the sky had started to darken during her run. The clouds were now gathering, and the moon was slowly disappearing behind them. What he hadn't noticed were the golden eyes that had been staring at the cottage.

Feeling Kayleigh's arms wrap around his waist, he covered her arms with his own.

"You and your beautiful white wolf will be mine one day," whispered Gautier.

"She is mine, and she has always been mine," the black wolf said, before he vanished into the darkness.

* * *

After spending every day together at the sapphire pool since his arrival, Kayleigh was ready for an adventure. The story Maw had told her about the crumbling castle on the other side of the mountain was so intriguing, she had begged Gautier to take her there. Unable to deny her anything, he soon found himself standing at the entrance to the tunnel.

"I'll go first," he said. "Stay close to me, Kayleigh."

As he stepped into the tunnel, he heard the scurrying of what he believed to be rats. With nothing but darkness ahead of him, he quickly illuminated the tunnel around them with a flick of his wrist. Tiny eyes reflected back at him before they scurried off through the cracks in the wall. Taking Kayleigh's hand, he pulled her next to him.

"Are you sure you want to do this?" he asked.

"I'm not afraid; are you?" she asked, with a tilt of her head.

"We'll see about that."

The illumination followed them as they made their way through the tunnel. Cobwebs hung from the tunnel's ceiling and water trickled down its walls. The deeper into the tunnel they went, the colder it got. Gautier could feel her hand quiver, and he knew that she was cold. Placing his arm around her, they continued to walk through the tunnel.

It seemed like there would be no end in sight until a small stream of light could be seen on the ceiling ahead of them. As they approached the light, they realized sunlight was streaming through a small opening to the outside.

"Are we at the end of the tunnel?" she asked.

"It appears to be a window to the outside," he replied.

Reaching the light, they saw what they thought was a dead end, but to its left were stone steps that went up. Gautier peered out the window to get a sense of where they were, but he could see nothing but the sea.

"The steps must lead to the castle," Kayleigh said, as she let go of Gautier's hand and quickly took the first three steps before he snatched her around the waist and pulled her back to stand beside him.

"Let me go first. Who knows what's up there." Kayleigh pursed her lips to keep from complaining. "Remember, this was your idea."

With their hands flat against the stones to keep their balance, the stairway spiraled around and around several times before they stepped out onto what seemed like a large balcony. Only a few stones remained that surrounded it, making it completely open to the rocks below. Tall grass grew among the cracks of the uneven stones, and rotten beams hung from the stones above them.

"Who lived here?" asked Gautier.

"It belonged to Lord and Lady Belmont. Maw told me a story she heard as a child about pirates that kidnapped their daughter. Her father and mother left the castle to search for her and never returned. With them gone, the castle fell to ruins."

Kayleigh walked about examining what was left of the stone walls. With the castle imbedded into the side of the mountain, it was left in full view of passing ships. Without the cover of trees, she knew it had left them vulnerable to attack with easy access from the rocks and no way to escape except through the narrow tunnel.

"It won't be long before it all tumbles to the rocks below."

The words had no sooner left Gautier's lips than the sound of something slamming into the stones above their heads caused him to whisk Kayleigh out of the way of falling debris. They watched as soil and small rocks followed by large blocks of stone covered with moss slammed into the stone floor.

"I think it best we leave this place," Gautier said, as he took hold of Kayleigh's hand.

As they made their way back to the steps that would lead them to the tunnel, Kayleigh caught a familiar scent. Stopping, she turned around to see if anyone was behind her.

"What is it?" asked Gautier.

"I thought I smelled musk."

"It is probably coming from the dirt and moss that fell at our feet. Now, let's leave this place before we find ourselves on the rocks below."

With both hands against the walls, they slowly made their way down the stone steps. Before Gautier could illuminate the tunnel, Kayleigh caught the heavy scent of musk and smoke. Pulling on his arm, she moved back toward the steps.

"It's here. The wolf is here," she whispered. "It must be in the tunnel."

"Get back up the steps, Kayleigh. Run to the far side of the balcony."

He turned and followed Kayleigh up the steps. Once out in the open, he pulled the dagger from his boot and readied himself for the wolf's attack. Prepared to hear the soft padding of its paws upon the stones, he was surprised to hear the solid sound of a man's boots climbing the steps. Glancing back over his shoulder to see Kayleigh with her back against the stone wall, he took a step back to be nearer to her.

As he turned back, a man stepped from the stairway's shadow. He was dressed in black with a human skull tied at his waist and carried a dagger in his hand. He was tall with white hair that fell to his shoulders. As he moved the dirty strands behind his ear, it exposed a ragged scar that ran across the bridge of his nose.

"Who are you, and what do you want?" barked Gautier.

"My name is Shauden, and I have come for the white wolf," he replied. "We have a history. She belongs to me."

"I don't belong to you," screamed Kayleigh. "Leave us!"

"I will not leave without you by my side." Shauden smiled and offered his outstretched hand to her.

"I will never go with you."

Feeling Kayleigh against his back, he reached for her hand.

"Leave this place while you still can," shouted Gautier. "The lady has given you her answer. She refuses your request."

"She refuses me only because she does not remember me. She need only think back to the day she foolishly walked alone in the forest. Had she not been running, I would have never caught the scent of her fear. I'm sure she will agree that the challenge of the chase is most exhilarating."

"It was you?" she gasped. "You bit my hand."

"She does remember me. Now, come with me," beckoned Shauden, as he smirked at Gautier. "I want to feel her bite against my neck."

"No, I will never go with you. My heart belongs to Gautier."

"You may have given him your heart, but your blood runs through my veins. You belong to me," Shauden replied.

"As long as there is breath in my body, she will never belong to you. Leave this place before you are unable to do so," warned Gautier.

Shauden threw his dagger to the ground and dropped to his knees. In an instant a black wolf stood before them. His eyes glowed with hatred as he paced back and forth preparing to strike.

Gautier pushed Kayleigh back and raised his dagger in defense as the black wolf leapt in the air. The force of the heavy wolf knocked the dagger from his hand as he fell to the ground. Trapped under the weight of the wolf, he tried to draw magic to his hands, but he was using too much energy to keep his ribs from being crushed by the wolf's hind paws. Feeling its hot breath against his face, he slammed his fists into the wolf's head and jabbed at its eyes with his thumbs.

Shaking its head, the wolf pulled back. Blood dripped from one eye as it lowered its head and focused on his prey. Lifting its paw, it felt something sharp against its neck. Unable to move, the wolf looked down to see blood running down Gautier's arm.

"Take my bite to your death," the white wolf screamed into his mind.

Her teeth sank deep into the black wolf's neck and ripped his head from his body. With the black wolf dead, her wolf staggered about with the realization of what she had done. It had been her first kill. The taste of his vile blood dripped from her mouth. Her vision slowly blurred, and she collapsed against the stones that were covered in his blood.

Gautier pushed the wolf's carcass from his body, and rushed to her wolf's side. Determined to get her wolf away from the sight of the dead wolf, he lifted her blood stained body and made his way to the steps that would take them back to the tunnel. Gautier carried her through the tunnel to the sapphire pool where he gently washed the blood from her fur. Seeing the life had vanished from her eyes, Gautier carried her back to her cottage.

After turning his back, she had finally shifted back into her human form. Without saying a word, she had dressed for bed and crawled under her blanket with her knees tucked against her chest. Unsure of what to do, he spent the night sitting at the foot of her bed listening to her cry and trying to calm her nightmares. It broke his heart to see the suffering, and for the first time, he was afraid of what she might say to him when she woke from her nightmares.

Three more days and nights passed before Kayleigh opened her eyes to find Gautier sitting on the floor by her bed with his head leaning back against its wooden frame. The slow steady sound of his breathing told her he was still sleeping. Pulling back her blanket, she crept from her bed trying not to wake him. Grabbing her shawl from its peg, she wrapped it around her shoulders as she made her way to the hearth. She could feel what was left of a fire he must have created sometime during the night. Sitting down in her chair, she gazed at the gentle man that owned her heart. After the horrors of what had happened at the crumbled castle, she knew she could never live without him.

"How long have you been awake?" he asked, as he stood and ran his hands over his face to wipe the sleep from his eyes.

"Long enough to make a decision."

"What decision is that?"

"I have decided I can't be afraid of Velsa or what might happen any longer. Gautier, I don't want to spend a day without you. I'm ready to go with you to Black Thistle Castle."

Gautier stood paralyzed by her words. He had expected her to withdraw from him or possibly flee. He never expected to hear she desired to return to his home.

"Did you hear me? Have you no response?"

"I'm not sure I heard you. Could you repeat the last few words again?"

As she stood, she offered him a smile as she slowly walked toward him.

"I'm ready to go with you to Black Thistle Castle."

He felt his heart race as he heard her words.

"Kayleigh, I was so afraid of what you would say when you woke this morning. I thought I would be nothing more than a reminder of what happened at the castle ruins, and you would send me away. To hear that you want to return to Black Thistle Castle with me, has me unable to express the joy that I feel."

"Do you think you might be able to show me?"

Gautier lifted her chin and kissed her forehead, the tip of her nose, and then claimed her lips with his own.

Chapter 10

After hugging Maw good-bye, Kayleigh boarded the Christaline's Slipper with her cheeks wet from tears and a heart filled with sadness. It wasn't until they had docked in Wood's Bay and Gautier had helped her mount the grey mare's back, that her sadness was replaced with nervous excitement.

They had ridden for what seemed like forever until they reached the shade of the Black Thistle Forest. For some reason, the name conjured visions of trolls hiding behind thorny bushes, and it caused her to stay even closer to Gautier's horse as they wove through the trees. Little did she know that a witch lived in the forest and had been seen gathering herbs near its edge earlier that day.

Taking advantage of the cool air, they slowed their pace until the thinly spaced trees offered them a view of the castle wall. Following Gautier's lead, Kayleigh gave her mare a kick with her heels and raced behind him toward the open gate. As Gautier crossed the drawbridge and entered the gate, he jumped from his horse. Lorcan was the first to see him and ran to greet him with a strong embrace.

"We've missed you and hoped for your return. Lord Heinrich and Lady Petula are to be married in three days, and Lord and Lady Larchmont should arrive the day after tomorrow," he blurted, as he collected the horse's reins.

Seeing another horse out of the corner of his eye, he looked up to see Kayleigh atop the grey mare. Grabbing the reins, he waited for Gautier to help her dismount.

"Let me be the first to welcome you to Black Thistle Castle," Lorcan said.

"It is nice to see you again," Kayleigh nervously replied, as she felt Gautier's comforting hand at her back.

"Lorcan, will you see to the horses? I need to find my brother."

Gautier guided Kayleigh to the castle's grand entrance. Stopping at the double doors, he took her hand and tenderly kissed her palm.

"This is your new home, Kayleigh. Do not be afraid. You will never be banished from its walls."

"Gautier, my home is wherever you are. I do not need walls to surround me as long as I have your arms to hold me."

After kissing the palm of her hand once more, he pushed open the heavy wooden doors to the Entry Hall and could hear voices coming from the Great Hall. Walking through the open doors with Kayleigh at his side, he saw his brother and Lady Petula standing in front of Godwine, the Head of the Black Thistle Council.

"My Lord, may I interrupt you?" shouted Gautier.

Seeing Gautier, he quickly dismissed Godwine and waited for his brother to approach him.

"My Lord . . . Lady Petula," Gautier said, as he stood at attention and bowed his head.

"I am pleased that you have finally come home, and I see that you have brought someone with you. Is this the woman you spoke of?" asked Gerwig.

"My Lord, this is Kayleigh Fallon."

Acknowledging the introduction, Kayleigh made a deep curtsy and bowed her head.

"Lord Heinrich . . . Lady Petula, it is an honor to meet you."

"Lorcan tells me that there will be a wedding," Gautier said, as he slapped his brother on the shoulder.

"Yes, she has willingly given her heart to me," Gerwig said, as he looked lovingly at Petula. "She will soon be Lady Heinrich and your little sister."

"I wish you both much happiness," Gautier replied.

"I am happier now that you have returned. I would have been disappointed if you had missed our wedding," replied Petula. "And Kayleigh, you must be tired after your long journey."

"It was long, and I find that I am quite tired."

"The Turret bedchamber is empty, and I will see that Faye comes to assist you. I think you will like it. The view from the window is heavenly," offered Petula.

"Thank you, My Lady."

"I'll see Kayleigh to her chamber," smiled Gautier. "I see Godwine is fidgeting at the door.

"We'll talk later after you've rested," replied Gerwig. "You can send in the old buzzard. He is full of wedding details that have made our heads spin."

Kayleigh pursed her lips trying not to laugh as Gautier led her away. She had found Gerwig and Petula to be delightful, and looked forward to getting to know them. For now, she longed for a warm bath and a good night's rest.

* * *

Gautier tapped his knuckle against the door and eagerly waited as he heard her light footsteps and the rustle of her skirt. When the door finally opened, he stood in silence for a moment forgetting to breathe.

"Gautier, say something."

"I'm sorry, your beauty has stolen the words I had prepared to say to you this morning."

"While you try to remember, come have tea with me."

"No, I want to take you someplace very special."

"Where?"

"It is a surprise. Take my hand and come with me."

Kayleigh walked by Gautier's side down two flights of stone steps and through a long hallway before stepping out into the morning light. To her surprise, Lorcan stood holding the reins of two horses dressed in the Black Thistle colors.

"We are going on another journey?" asked Kayleigh. "I have barely recovered from the last."

"Just a short ride," he replied.

Gautier led her to a wooden box that had been placed alongside the mare she had ridden from Woods Village. The mare had been groomed and purple ribbons had been tied in her mane. She felt Gautier take her arm as she lifted her skirt to step up onto the box. After mounting her mare, she took the reins from Lorcan and waited for Gautier to mount his horse.

"Are you ready?" he asked.

Kayleigh nodded as she nudged her mare to follow him.

The sun was warm, but a gentle breeze made the ride enjoyable. Not knowing what to expect, she was thrilled to see a meadow filled with wildflowers ahead of them.

"This is lovely," she sighed. "I love the scent of wildflowers."

"I remember," he replied.

Riding through the meadow, Kayleigh could see lavender growing within a cluster of rocks up ahead of them, and she noticed the sweet fragrance drifting on the breeze. As they got closer to the rocks, she discovered what she had seen from her bedchamber window was not a field of lavender flowers, but it was a canyon filled with rows and rows of lavender.

Gautier could see the surprise on her face and delighted in seeing her smile.

"It's beautiful," she cried.

"It is even more spectacular from the bottom."

"From the bottom?"

"Yes," he laughed. "There is a narrow path on the other side of those rocks that will lead us to the bottom." Kayleigh eagerly followed Gautier to the path. "Be careful, it is very narrow."

At the bottom, they were greeted by two very small young women with long lavender hair. Gautier quickly dismounted and knelt down to be eye-level with the women.

"Is everything ready?" he asked, as quietly as he could.

Seeing their smiles, he stood and helped Kayleigh off the back of her mare. Taking her hand, he could hardly control his excitement.

"I have something to show you, but we will have to walk. The lavender is too thick to ride the horses."

"I don't mind walking."

As they walked between the rows of lavender, Kayleigh took in the beautiful scenery and inhaled the wonderful scent. Small stone cottages with thatched roofs were scattered about the canyon. Water fell from the walls of the canyon making streams of crystal clear water that fed a sparkling pond surrounded by trees full of pink buds. After a butterfly landed on her arm, she felt as though she had entered a magical dream world. It was unlike any place she had ever seen.

"See that waterfall? That is where we are going," he said.

Gautier helped Kayleigh over the smooth rocks of a stream and led her to the base of a waterfall that was so sheer it looked like a thin sheet of ice.

"I have a surprise for you behind the water, follow me."

Kayleigh carefully maneuvered her body between the water and the rocks. At first, the feel of her damp skirt had disappointed her, but it was all forgotten when she saw the flicker of candlelight. A small cave hidden behind the waterfall had been filled with flickering candles.

"Gautier, it is beautiful."

Taking her hands in his, he lifted them to his lips. After kissing her palms, he slowly bent down on one knee.

"Kayleigh, since the moment I saw you, my heart has belonged to you. You have brought meaning to my life, and it has been brightened each day by the sound of your voice. What I am trying to say, Kayleigh, is that I love you. As I kneel before you, I ask you to take me as yours and yours alone."

Tears welled in Kayleigh's eyes as she knelt before Gautier.

"Gautier, I love you. My heart and my love will always belong to you. I am honored to take you as mine and mine alone."

Gautier fumbled with a pouch at his waist before he was able to drop a ring onto the palm of his hand.

"This ring belonged to my mother. The band is engraved with the thorns of the thistles and an amethyst stone that symbolized my mother's love for the purple thistles that surround Black Thistle Castle. For me, the thorns represent my promise to protect you, and the purple stone represents the memory of this day in the Wispet Canyon."

He took her hand and slowly placed the ring upon her finger.

"It is beautiful. I will cherish it always. It will be like our love, always and forever."

$$* * *$$

Velsa had seen the troop of horses led by Gautier as they escorted Lord and Lady Larchmont to Black Thistle. The wind had been full of their arrival and the preparations for the wedding. The news of Gautier's return had been hidden from her, but the sight of him sitting upon his horse had stolen her breath away. It had been all she had thought about as she made her way to Peaks View.

Seeing the sheep, she knew she was close to Thurston Moxley's barn. He had promised her wool from the first shearing in return for the elixir to cure the sores on his son's legs. The sores were gone, and she was ready to collect the wool.

Hearing a rhythmic pounding, she found Thurston at the corner of his cottage chopping wood. She decided to give him a shout to let him know that she was coming his way. She had found it wasn't good to startle a man holding an axe.

"Mistress Velsa, have you come to collect your wool?" he asked, as he looked at the strange color of her hair and furrowed his brows. The last time he had seen her it had been as golden as flax. "Are you well?"

"Never mind . . . you promised to have the wool ready for me, and I am here to collect it," yawned Velsa.

"It is in the barn. I'll fetch it for you."

Velsa watched as he made his way to the barn. Before he could return, the cottage door opened and out stepped Genevieve. She was half Thurston's age with a high pitched voice that never seemed to stop talking. She would rattle one question after another without waiting long enough to hear the answer to her last ridiculous question.

"I wasn't sure that was you, Velsa. What have you done to your hair? Have you been sick? I have heard that Bicker's Illness can turn your hair grey. Is that what happened? Did you come down with Bicker's Illness? Oh, my friend, Bethany, told me once that frog urine mixed with moss and black mushrooms will cure Bicker's Illness. I've never tried it. Well, I have never had Bicker's Illness and never had the need to cure it."

Genevieve took a much needed breath as Thurston walked toward them carrying two burlap bags of wool.

"Oh, I know what I wanted to ask you. Your grey hair distracted me, and I started talking about Bicker's Illness. I get distracted easily. Everyone tells me that I get distracted easily."

"Genevieve, what did you want to ask me?" Velsa quickly interrupted her.

"Did you hear about the wedding? Lord Gautier is getting married. It will be a grand affair."

"No, Lord Heinrich is getting married to Lady Petula."

"No . . . No . . . Velsa, I know what I heard. Lord Gautier is going to get married two days after the big wedding. I can't remember her name. Oh! I remember her name. Her name is Lady Fallon. Yes, it is Lady Fallon. I am sure of it."

"You are confused. Lord Heinrich is marrying Lady Petula Larchmont. It is their wedding that you have heard about."

"I know what I heard. Don't look at me like I'm the crazy one." Genevieve turned and stormed back to her cottage leaving Velsa exhausted from all the chatter. "I know what I heard."

The door slammed and Thurston looked from the door to Velsa and shrugged his shoulders.

"She gets something set in her mind and there is no changing it, but she is a kind soul. She has been a good mate. I can't complain," sighed Thurston. "Are you needing any help with the wool?"

"No, I have a wagon up the hill," she replied. "Go see after Genevieve. I'm sure she needs your comforting words."

Thurston sat the bags down and headed for the cottage door. As he entered the cottage, Velsa could hear Genevieve crying before Thurston closed the door. Grabbing the bags, she vanished back to her own little cottage.

Dropping the bags of wool in the corner, she pondered what Genevieve had said about Gautier and Lady Fallon. She knew of the village gossip. She had been the subject of many of the rumors that lingered in Peaks Village and Primrose Pond. People would gossip about anything, anyone, and everything; however, she found most of it to be untrue.

Snatching her book of spells, she fanned through the pages. The pages seemed thicker and the book much heavier. Placing it back on the table, she placed her hands on either side of it.

"Give me a spell that will seek the truth," she said as she stroked its leather cover.

The cover flew open, and the pages fluttered back and forth. Once it stopped, she looked down at a truth spell her mother had written when she was a young girl. As she began to read the words, it slowly faded away. In its place, one word after another written in thick black ink replaced her mother's spell.

Whisper, Whisper in their ear

Tell the truth to someone dear

Whisper, Whisper in my ear

Let me hear it loud and clear

Velsa snapped her fingers and a flame glowed from her black candle. She took a deep breath and repeated the spell. Expecting something to happen, she was disappointed when she felt nothing. The page before her fluttered, and she felt something stroke the side of her face.

"We seek your blood in payment for your spell," a raspy voice whispered in her ear. *"You must feed the darkness with your blood."*

Opening her black chest, she reached in and withdrew the dagger she had used before. Cutting her palm, she let the blood drip onto the book's parchment. The words written in black ink quickly absorbed her blood. Staring down at the dark red words, she repeated the spell.

Whisper, Whisper in their ear

Tell the truth to someone dear

Whisper, Whisper in my ear

Let me hear it loud and clear

Finished, the flame of the candle disappeared. The smoke that lingered swirled up into the air and out through the crack in the door.

Velsa stumbled away from her table to her chair by the hearth. Feeling dizzy, she sat down and closed her eyes to wait for the message of truth to return to her.

* * *

The festivities were well under way when Gautier and Kayleigh entered the Great Hall. It had been so long since she had been around so many people, she held tightly to his arm for fear she would fall.

"We need to speak to Lord and Lady Larchmont. They are our guests, and it would be rude if we ignored them," he whispered.

"Lead the way, My Lord, but don't let go of my hand," she replied.

"Never."

As they approached Gerwig, they were stopped by Derora.

"I haven't had a chance to meet the lady on your arm, and it is rumored that she has accepted your proposal. Will there be an announcement this evening?" she asked.

"Derora, this is Kayleigh Fallon. Kayleigh, this is Derora. She has been like a mother to me since my mother's passing."

"My dear, you look lovely this evening," offered Derora. Seeing Kayleigh lift her other hand to grasp Gautier's arm, she noticed the ring upon her finger. "I see you are wearing the amethyst ring that belonged to his mother."

"If it will quiet your chatter, I do not deny the rumors. I have proposed. She has accepted me, but tonight we celebrate my brother and Petula," he sternly replied. "Afford us this small secret for a few days. It is their night. After they are wed tomorrow, there is time enough to announce our intentions."

"As you wish, but your proposal is on the tip of everyone's tongue," she whispered, as she walked away.

* * *

The scent of smoke woke Velsa from her sleep. With her eyes still closed, she twisted her head to relieve the stiffness in her neck. Hearing the bones in her neck pop, she opened her eyes to see a small wisp of smoke directly in front of her.

"Do you bring me the truth that I requested?"

The smoke playfully swirled about her head. Frustrated, Velsa swatted at it until it settled on her shoulder.

"Tell me what you have heard," she demanded.

"The whispers are true. Gautier proposed to Lady Fallon within the Wispet Canyon. The Wispets prepared a candlelit cave behind a sheer waterfall for them. She has accepted, and she wears his amethyst ring upon her hand. They will be married soon. You have requested the truth, and it has been brought to you," a deep voice replied.

Velsa screamed as she wrapped her arms around her waist. The words set her soul on fire. Trying to elude the pain, she thrashed about as she tore at her flesh. Looking down at the blood on her hands, she dropped to the floor. Her screams were the last things she heard before she felt the darkness wrap its arms around her and take her from the pain.

Chapter 11

The wedding preparations were complete. The Great Hall had been filled with flowers and candles. Ribbons of blue, gold, green, and purple hung from its heavy wooden beams. The stained glass windows that lined one wall spilled colorful beams of light upon the stone floor. The simple wooden altar had been covered with a purple banner embroidered with gold feathers surrounded by lavender thistles.

With the ceremony ready to start, the crowd was beginning to gather in the hall. Krega and his mate, Aderyn, stood near the back of the hall with Cadfan, Henwas, and Darach. Derora huddled with Ida, Iris, and Ingrid as they admired the decorations created by their magic. Godwine waited impatiently at the doorway to the hall. His constant sigh sent Gautier in search of his brother.

Kayleigh watched as Petula's mother tightened the laces of her daughter's gown. It was unlike anything she had ever seen. The rich gold satin shimmered with hues of deep blue and purple. It had been made to pay homage to both the colors of Featherstone and Black Thistle, and the bodice had been embroidered with golden thistles. Ella and Annalee had curled her hair and it hung in soft ringlets against her back. With her laces tied, she was ready to meet Gerwig.

The crowd hushed as soft music began to play. Godwine entered the hall and slowly made his way to the altar followed by Gerwig. With Kayleigh at his side, Gautier walked behind his brother. After delivering her to Derora's side, he took his place beside his brother at the altar. Gautier heard his brother's faint gasp as Petula entered the hall with her parents. As they approached, Gerwig nervously clutched his hands behind his back.

"Take a breath, brother. She is almost here," Gautier whispered.

Gautier watched as Lord Larchmont placed Petula's hand upon his brother's palm. It was a symbolic gesture, and it saddened him that Kayleigh's parents would not be there to do the same.

Turning to face Godwine, the music stopped as he opened a small leather bound book and began to speak.

"Today we come to witness the joining of Petula and Gerwig for all eternity. Their love for one another bloomed slowly like the petals of a flower that welcomes the sun. It grew with trust, respect, and kindness. Their love has been proven worthy. Lord Gerwig Heinrich, do you pledge your trust, honor, love, and protection to Petula forever more?"

"I will, forever more," declared Gerwig.

"Lady Petula Larchmont, do you pledge your trust, honor, love, and protection to Gerwig forever more?"

"I will, forever more," Petula softly replied.

Godwine looked out over the crowd that filled the hall.

"Do you pledge your trust, honor, love, and protection to Gerwig and Petula?"

In unison they responded, "We will, forever more."

Godwine turned and lifted a cord woven with blue, gold, purple, and green threads from the altar.

"This cord has been woven with the colors of their families. It symbolizes the joining of two hearts that will beat forever as one," declared Godwine as he wrapped the cord around their wrists.

Godwine stood with his arms raised as he looked down at Gerwig and Petula.

"It is with great honor that I declare Lord and Lady Heinrich united for all eternity. My Lord, you may kiss your bride."

Cheers filled the hall as Gerwig bent down and kissed Petula.

Gautier waited for Godwine to untie the cord before he congratulated his brother with a warm embrace.

"May I offer a kiss to my new sister," asked Gautier.

Seeing his brother nod, he kissed the tear from Petula's cheek.

"May you only shed tears of happiness, little sister," he whispered in her ear.

Stepping back to allow the crowd to surround Gerwig and Petula, he searched for Kayleigh. He found her standing in the corner wiping tears from her eyes. As he took her hand, he was glad to see her eyes brighten.

"Let's find someplace quiet where I can watch your wolf run," he begged. "I want her to enjoy her new home."

Seeing her smile, they ran from the hall.

* * *

The celebrations had finally stopped. Lord and Lady Larchmont were on their way back to Featherstone, and the castle had returned to its usual quiet manner. Gautier felt it was time to speak with his brother about his own wedding. Kayleigh wanted nothing more than a simple wedding with Gerwig, Petula, and Derora in attendance. They had both chosen the turret's balcony to say their vows. It offered a distant view of Wispet Canyon, and with the backdrop of a colorful sunset, they thought it was the perfect place.

After seeing Ella carrying the breakfast tray for Gerwig and Petula, he had stopped her to carry a message to his brother. Standing in the Council Chamber, he paced back and forth waiting for him to arrive.

"What's this urgent request that has pulled me from my marriage bed?" bellowed Gerwig.

"I beg your pardon, My Lord, but Kayleigh and I would like you and Petula to witness our marriage vows, tomorrow."

"Tomorrow?"

"It will be nothing more than a simple ceremony with you, Petula, and Derora in attendance. She has agreed to be mine, and we are eager to have the words spoken."

"If that is what you desire, you shall have it. Do you love her?"

"With all my heart, Gerwig. She is everything to me."

"Then, where shall we meet you?"

"We have chosen to say our vows on the turret's balcony at sunset."

"You have my blessing. If there is nothing else, I will return to Petula."

* * *

When Kayleigh had opened the door dressed in a simple green dress and a ribbon woven in her braid, Derora just laughed as she closed the door.

"This will never do," hissed Derora. "This is your wedding day."

"It is a simple wedding between two people that love each other. We need nothing more than the words we will say to each other."

"Let me do this one thing for you. It will be my gift. You can't refuse a gift from me on your wedding day."

"I will accept this one gift and nothing more."

Kayleigh stood perfectly still as Derora began to chant. Her green dress suddenly fell from her body to the floor. Small flickering lights darted in and out of the fabric until the dress glowed a deep purple. Derora snapped her fingers, and the dress drifted from the floor. Hanging in midair, Kayleigh saw a purple gown of crushed velvet with sheer trumpet sleeves. Gold ribbon adorned a belt that tied at the waist and hung to the floor. It was the most beautiful dress she had ever seen.

"Let's get you dressed," sighed Derora. "I'm sure Gautier is waiting at your door."

Finally dressed and adorned to Derora's satisfaction, she waited silently on the balcony for Gautier. Not hearing the door open, she looked up in surprise to see Gautier standing before her.

"You look beautiful," he said, as he moved to stand beside her.

Godwine followed closely behind him and ushered Gerwig, Petula and Derora to stand behind him.

"Are we ready?" asked Godwine.

Gautier and Kayleigh smiled at each other and replied yes at the same time.

"Today, we come to witness . . ."

Even though Godwine was speaking, Kayleigh and Gautier were captured by the love in each other's eyes and heard nothing but the beating of their own hearts. The gentle touch of Godwine's hand broke the spell, and Gautier looked at him.

"Gautier, repeat your vow?"

"Get on with it," his brother added.

"I will, forever more," replied Gautier.

"And, I do as well," Kayleigh said, as she wiped a tear from her eye.

Not waiting for Godwine, Gerwig offered his response, "We all will, forever more."

Kayleigh was the first to laugh which caused Godwine to mumble to himself. Clearly flustered, Godwine snapped his book closed and waited for silence. After a few moments, he continued.

"It is my honor to declare Lady Kayleigh and Lord Gautier united for all eternity. Gautier, you may kiss your bride."

Gautier brushed the side of Kayleigh's face with the back of his hand and whispered, "I love you."

As he touched his lips to hers, he heard the others cheering their congratulations. Pulling back to look into her eyes, he discovered they had been left alone with a ring of white rose petals at their feet.

"What is this?" asked Gautier.

"Look, it leads into the chamber," laughed Kayleigh. "Is this Derora's doing?"

Stepping into the bedchamber, they saw a trail of rose petals leading to the door. Making their way to the door, they opened it to find more petals scattered along the dim hallway. Curious as to where it would lead them, they followed it.

Standing amongst the last of the rose petals, Gautier opened the door to find a bedchamber filled with flickering candles.

"It's beautiful," sighed Kayleigh.

As they stepped through the door, they were greeted by Faye.

"My Lord, I am here to help My Lady prepare for bed."

Kayleigh smiled at Gautier and then followed Faye into the bathing chamber.

Gautier stood with his hand against the thick beam of the mantle wearing a sleeping tunic that had been left for him on the bed. At first, he had hesitated to bother with it, but when Faye walked from the bathing chamber, he was glad he had done so.

The sound of Kayleigh's bare feet against the wooden floor made him look from the fire that burned in the hearth to the shy smile she offered him. Her hair hung unadorned in soft waves about her shoulders to her waist. As his eyes drifted over her sheer white sleeping gown, he yearned to untie the ribbon that would let it fall from her body.

Walking toward her, he tried to remember the sweet words he had planned to say to her on their wedding night. He had rehearsed the words over and over in his mind, but seeing her standing before him, they had suddenly been stolen from his mind. As he brushed her hair from her shoulder, he saw her eyes close and felt her lean into his hand.

"You are so lovely," he whispered, as he gently kissed her neck.

He left one kiss after another against her neck and across her shoulder until he felt the silkiness of the ribbon brush against his lips.

"You are my first, Gautier," she sighed, as she felt the warmth of each kiss against her skin.

Hearing her words, he put his mouth to her ear, "My heart and my love will always belong to you. I am honored to take you as mine and mine alone, and I will spend the rest of my days comforting you, protecting you, and loving you."

Feeling her reach for the ribbon, he stepped back and watched as she pulled it from her shoulder letting the sheer sleeping gown caress her body as it fell in a puddle at her feet. He gasped at the sight of her beautiful body and felt his own body react from the pleasure. Lifting her up in his arms, he carried her to their bed and rested her head against the soft linen pillows. After pulling his tunic over his head and dropping it to the floor, he entered their bed and pulled her against his body.

"Kayleigh, I will always love you," whispered Gautier.

* * *

Kayleigh was the first to wake. She yawned as she snuggled against Gautier's body, and sighed as she felt his fingers gently caress her back. Longing for more, she feathered kisses across his chest.

"You're awake." Gautier smiled and brushed the hair from her face. Leaning forward, he kissed the top of her head.

"Good morning, my love," Kayleigh said, as she brought her hand to her mouth to cover another yawn.

"I think you will find it is long past morning. Did you sleep well?"

Kayleigh pushed the soft bed linens back and moved to straddle his waist. Placing her finger at the base of his neck, she slowly ran it down through the soft dark hairs of his chest. Gautier could see the blush on her cheeks and the tangles in her hair. It brought visions of their love making to his mind, and he needed more of her.

"Did we sleep? I feel as though I just closed my eyes, and a new day has begun." She smiled as she playfully lifted her hair from her neck and shoulders to expose her nakedness. "Or, is this only a dream?"

Delighted by her boldness, he watched as she slowly lowered her body against his own. Unable to wait any longer, he claimed her mouth and felt her explore his mouth with her tongue.

A sudden rap upon the door caused them to pause.

Please leave our door, thought Gautier. Now is not the time for visitors.

Kayleigh looked at Gautier and jerked away from him. Sitting up she stared down at him with a confused expression.

Again, they heard the rap upon the door, as well as, Faye's voice.

"My Lord, Lord Heinrich has sent me with a breakfast tray."

Pursing his lips as he left their bed, Gautier snatched his tunic from the floor and pulled it over his head as he made his way to the door. Looking over his shoulder, he waited until Kayleigh pulled the bed linens up to cover her naked body before he opened it.

"My Lord, I am sorry for the intrusion. I have brought you a breakfast tray from Lord and Lady Heinrich. They thought you would prefer breakfast in your chamber," she shyly said, keeping her eyes on the floor and making her way to the small table in front of the hearth.

"I will offer my thanks to my brother in person when I see him," Gautier gruffly replied.

"Are you in need of water for the bathing tub or wood for the fire?" asked Faye.

Gautier waved his hand and a fire appeared in the hearth.

"As you can see, I have no need of wood for the fire, and filling the bathing tub will be just as easy."

Feeling flustered, Faye lifted the hem of her skirt and hurried through the open door.

After kicking the door closed with his bare foot, he turned to find Kayleigh wrapped in bed linens holding a sweet cake to her mouth.

"I see that you are hungry for more than what our bed has to offer."

I am famished, My Lord.

Gautier's mouth hung open as he tried to make sense of hearing her thoughts in his mind.

It appears we have acquired something new from our marriage bed. Come join me before I eat every one of these warm sweet cakes.

* * *

After recovering from the discovery of their new connection, Gautier and Kayleigh had spent the day together making a game of communicating in silence. Being a curious soul, Kayleigh wondered if the same would be true with her wolf. Eager to find out, they made their way back to their bedchamber to wait for the moon to rise in the sky.

Gautier could feel this jaw tighten as he heard the popping sounds as she shifted before he saw Kayleigh's wolf standing before him. As her wolf looked up at him, he noticed something different. Her eyes were no longer a bright golden color. They had changed to a mesmerizing crystal blue that mimicked Kayleigh's eyes in her human form.

"Your wolf's eyes have changed color. They are no longer golden. It appears our marriage bed has offered you another gift," he said. Kneeling down, he ran his fingers through her thick white fur and pressed his face against hers.

"Are you ready to run, my little wolf?" he asked.

I am ready. Can you hear me? Can you hear me in your mind?

Yes, I can hear you.

Did you do this, Gautier? Is this your magic?

I did nothing. It must be a gift from our union.

I wonder if I can hear you if we are far from each other?

There is only one way to find out.

Kayleigh's wolf walked by Gautier's side through the castle hallways. When she saw Lady Petula leaving the library and closing the door, she slowed and hid herself behind Gautier.

There is no need to hide, my love. Lady Petula knows you are a wolf shifter. She has been eager to see your white wolf.

Hearing Gautier's words comforted her fears, and she sat quietly waiting as Lady Petula made her way toward her. After greeting Gautier, Petula bent down and stroked the fur along her back.

"Your wolf is beautiful, Kayleigh. I understand you are going for a run. I must warn you to be careful of the hunter's traps in the forest. They are well hidden and waiting to snap closed around a paw or a foot."

Kayleigh could hear Gautier laughing and watched as he kissed the back of Petula's hand before she excused herself from their presence.

It was the sound of the gate opening that made her heart pound. She looked up at Gautier and waited for him to allow her release. Seeing the nod of his head, she raced for the shelter of the trees.

Enjoy your run but be careful. There is danger in the forest.

* * *

The forest was cool, and the thick canopy of the trees let very little of the moonlight filter between its branches. Gautier found it difficult to maneuver in the darkness and had decided to sit down on a hollow log to wait for Kayleigh's return. As he lifted his hand to produce a flame, he heard the snapping of twigs and the sound of something dragging against the floor of the forest.

Is that you, Kayleigh?

The sound of rapid breathing filled his ears. Waving his hand, he produced a flame set among a few rocks that he hoped would scare off whatever animal had found him.

Is there trouble, Gautier? I am just beyond the stream. I will find you.

Be careful, I do not know what creature has found me.

The crunching and snapping of twigs continued as tall shadows grew among the trees. Fearing it was some spirit of darkness that danced among the forest, he was shocked to see an old woman wearing a long cape step from the darkness. Her face was scared, and her hair hung in two loose braids. He could hear her rapid breathing and the pounding of her heart.

"What brings you to the dark forest alone?" the woman asked.

He looked at the woman that stood before him. There was something familiar about her eyes, but he couldn't figure out where he had seen her before.

"It is clear that you don't recognize me. I am not surprised. Sadly, I have changed. You see, life has been cruel to me."

"Who are you and why do you creep about the forest at night?"

"I walk the forest at night to keep from dreaming. It is the dreams of a lost love that haunt me."

I am almost there. I can hear you.

Be careful, Kayleigh. Someone has come upon me, and I am not sure of her intent.

Gautier could hear the soft padding of Kayleigh's wolf before she entered the small clearing to stand beside him. Her presence caught the woman by surprise causing her to step back and lean her hand against a nearby tree to keep from falling.

"You . . . are a wolf shifter. I find this very strange. There has been no wolf shifter's on this island since a rogue black wolf hid in our forests. He terrorized many before his alpha chased him from the island. I have known of no others since then."

"She is my mate and no danger to anyone, unless attacked."

Gautier watched as the woman grabbed her heart and began to sway. He took a step toward her but stopped when he saw her raise her hand and shake her head to deny his help.

"Your mate? You have taken a wolf shifter as your mate? You could find no other to claim your heart?"

Gautier took another step toward the old woman with fists clenched.

"Watch your words, woman! She is my only love, and I will not have you demean her."

"I see, a love like no other has captured your heart."

The woman turned to leave. Hesitating for a moment, she looked back over her shoulder at the white wolf and then up at Gautier.

"Enjoy her while you can."

Gautier recognized the look of sadness in her eyes. He had seen it before and felt sorry for the old woman. As he watched her step further into the shadows, she seemed to disappear.

Who was that woman?

I don't know, Kayleigh, but I think it best we return to the castle.

* * *

Bright purple sparks ricocheted around her cottage as she tore off her cape and collapsed onto her cot. The visions of Gautier and the white wolf filled her mind, and she pounded her head with her hands to try and make them leave.

"How could he?" screamed Velsa. "How could he mate with that mongrel?"

Looking up at the smoldering herbs that hung from her ceiling, she had an idea.

"This will be fun!"

Kicking off her boots, she leaned back against her feather pillow. Closing her eyes, she called to the darkness to enter her dreams.

"I have work to do, and I need you to show me the way."

Chapter 12

As Astra opened her cottage door, she noticed everything before her seemed brighter than usual, and she raised her hand to shelter her eyes from its intensity. She winced at the high-pitched sound of the breeze that brushed against her face, but it was the strange shimmering auras that caused her to quickly close her door. She knew what it all meant. A vision was coming. She struggled to reach her bed before the vision claimed her body and her mind. The moment she touched her coverlet, the room began to spin, and she fell to her knees. Clutching the soft fabric, she drew it to her face as she slipped to the floor. Her eyelids fluttered as a vision was slowly revealed.

A light fog surrounded a woman as she paced back and forth in front of a cluttered table while screaming obscenities. Dried herbs hung from the beams of the ceiling and shook as she waved her hands above her head. "You have betrayed me. You have betrayed me," the woman shouted. "You have given to her what you should have given to me." Covering her face with her hands, she collapsed into her chair. "I promise that you will feel my revenge for all of it."

The vision slowly faded away, and it was replaced by the scent of lavender before another vision appeared.

A man and a woman walked among rows of lavender until they reached a waterfall as sheer as ice. As they crept behind the water, the warmth of flickering candles surrounded them. A man dropped to one knee and offered a ring to the woman that stood before him. She dropped to her knees before him with the ring upon her finger.

The short vision faded, and Astra could see her body floating above a cool dark canyon. The cool air was slowly replaced by the smell of smoke as a new vision appeared.

A woman stood at the edge of a canyon filled with lavender pointing her finger at a beautiful woman that wore a crown. As she screamed words of hatred, hail began to fall and lightning filled the sky. She stood laughing as she watched flames burst from the canyon's floor. The women of the canyon ran for their lives as a fierce wind caused the stone cottages to crumble. Off in the distance, a shimmering lavender ring of light appeared beyond the trees. One by one, the women raced for the ring and jumped into the light. As the flames died down, the black remains of the canyon brought a smile to the woman's face as she turned her back on the destruction and walked away.

The horrible vision finally faded away, and Astra's body flinched as the cool darkness was replaced with the sound of screaming. The vision appeared to be hidden until the light from flames made the vision appear.

Smoke filled the hallways of a castle as flames leapt from its walls. People ran screaming as an army tried to protect them from the blasts of light that came from a woman's hands. A banner bearing the boar and thistle fell from its staff as flames engulfed it. Witches filled the sky above the castle as bursts of light were thrown back and forth at each other. One by one, the witches fell from the sky.

The vision faded into darkness, and the screams gave way to an eerie silence.

Astra slowly opened her eyes and raised her trembling body from the floor. Unable to stand, she fell back onto her bed. Her visions had been filled with hatred, death, and destruction. Tears fell from her eyes as she realized her sister had caused all of it. Forcing herself to stand, she knew she had to warn the Wispet Queen and Lord Heinrich. Somehow, her sister had to be stopped, and she feared it would mean her death to do so.

An unannounced visit to Black Thistle from Astra was rare. Hearing she had asked to meet with him and Gautier, Gerwig was certain it meant trouble. As he entered the Council Chamber, he could see the look of fear in Astra's eyes. Seeing her stumble as she tried to curtsey, he reached for her arm to help her stand.

"I think it would be good if we sit," he smiled, as he helped her to a chair and sat down beside her. He could see the trembling of her hands and covered them with his own. "I have sent for Gautier, and he will be here soon. There is no need to speak until he arrives."

Astra looked up and tried to smile. A quivering bottom lip was all she could offer him before tears threatened to fall from her eyes. Hearing the echo of Gautier's boots, she stilled as she waited for his arrival. As Gautier entered the Council Chamber, it was Astra's fragile state that caused him to kneel before her.

"What has happened?" asked Gautier.

"I have had a horrible vision," she replied, as she tried to wipe the tears from her face.

"Astra, can you tell us what you have seen?" asked Gerwig.

"A curse will be cast upon the Wispet Canyon, and all of the Wispets will be driven away. The canyon will be filled with flames and everything within it will die."

"Have you spoken with the Wispet Queen," asked Gerwig.

"I have come from the canyon. She is preparing her people for an escape through her portal. She has decided not to wait until the curse is upon them."

"Is that all you have seen," Gautier asked, knowing full-well that she had more to tell them.

"Also, a war is coming to this castle, and it is a war that you will not be able to win. Your castle will be demolished. A war between witches will cause many to die."

"I believe I know the answer to my question, but I must ask it. Who will bring this war?" asked Gautier.

"My sister will bring the war. I have seen her stand at the edge of the canyon and outside your castle wall. The war is coming unless you can stop her."

"You must take care of this," ordered Gerwig. "You brought her to this castle, and it is your responsibility to stop her."

"I know that she can become very angry, but I have never known her to cause someone harm," replied Gautier.

"She knows of your visit to the Wispet Canyon, and the moments you spent behind the waterfall. This destruction is her revenge against your betrayal."

"End this," growled Gerwig. "I want you to end this. If it means her death, so be it. I want this to end."

* * *

After leaving the castle, Astra rode her pony through the forest toward Velsa's cottage. She knew she had been warned to stay away from Gautier and the castle, but after seeing the vision, the warning she offered them far outweighed what might happen to herself by Velsa's magic.

Seeing the glow of candlelight through the cottage window, Astra dismounted her pony and approached Velsa's door. Taking a deep breath, she rapped on the wooden door and waited. The door swung open, but she could still feel a barrier before her.

"Enter," yelled her sister, as a slight ripple could be seen in the barrier before it disappeared.

Astra stepped inside her sister's cottage. There before her stood the woman she had seen at the edge of the canyon and outside the wall at Black Thistle Castle. She no longer resembled the likeness of her sister. Her hair was grey, and her skin was darkened with age spots. She heard herself gasp when she saw the claw marks covered with a thick salve that marred each side of her sister's face.

"Who has harmed you?" asked Astra.

"No one has harmed me. It was merely a bit of rage that got out of hand, but the darkness is healing me," replied Velsa. "It is nothing to concern yourself over."

She stared at Astra and waited for her to speak. Tired of her silence, she waved her hand toward the door. As the door slammed, Astra's body jerked in response.

"Out with it," groaned Velsa. "You must have something to say or you wouldn't be here."

"I am here to tell you that I have seen a number of unsettling visions," Astra nervously announced.

"What kind of unsettling visions?"

"I have seen a vision of horrible destruction against the Wispet Canyon and Black Thistle Castle. In this vision, you have caused the destruction, and . . ."

"And?"

"And, I have gone to warn the Wispet Queen, Lord Heinrich, and Gautier."

Astra could feel the air around her begin to cool, and she knew she was in danger.

"Did I not warn you to stay away from Gautier? Did I not tell you what I would do to you if you ignored my warning?"

Astra took a step back, but as hard as she tried, she could not take another. She tried to pull her magic to protect herself, but she could only feel it draining from the tips of her fingers. Standing paralyzed, she watched as Velsa walked toward her with clenched fists glowing a deep purple. She could smell Velsa's putrid salve, and it stung her eyes as her sister leaned toward her.

"First, I had to deal with the hurt of Gautier's betrayal. Now, I must deal with your betrayal," she forced through clenched teeth. "You will pay for what you have done."

Velsa placed her gnarled finger under Astra's chin and looked deep into her eyes. One by one, she pulled the visions from her mind. As the last one faded, Velsa laughed.

"You have missed the best one, my dear. It is a shame that you will not be around to witness what you have seen."

"Please don't do it, Velsa. So many innocents will die."

Velsa snapped her fingers, and Astra's voice was silenced.

"I promised to send you away, didn't I. Let me think. Where shall I send you? I could send you to the pits of the Underworld, bury you in a chest at sea, or lock you away on the mountain."

Astra knew of the mountain and the creature that lived there. To be sent there would mean her certain death, and she silently begged the stars to save her.

Dropping her hand from Astra's chin, she bent down and kissed her on the lips.

"This might hurt a little bit, but a wicked spell isn't worth much if it doesn't have a little sting."

Taking a step backward, she turned her back on Astra and began flicking purple sparks from her fingers. After clearing her throat, Velsa spun around and faced her sister. Slowly she lifted her hand, pointed her finger at her, and began to chant.

You are banished to the mountain
Locked away from my sight
To live with your betrayal
In the darkness of the night

You take no magic with you
You take no body too
A mere ghost of an existence
Is all I offer you

A challenge I will grant you
An escape for you to earn
Collect one thousand items
If you're lucky you'll return

Your Mountain cave is waiting
And a list for you to find
Go quickly little sister
Before I change my mind

Velsa's evil smile was the last thing Astra saw before she felt her body vanish from her sister's cottage and land upon the crumbled rocks of the creature's mountain. She looked down at the translucent skin of her hands and began to cry, "I am lost forever."

* * *

Not long after Astra was banished from her sight, Velsa heard Gautier shouting her name. Angered by the noise he was making, she yanked open her door to confront him.

"What has brought you to my cottage? You have thrown me away and no longer have any need for me. After all, you have found another."

"It was you . . . that I saw in the forest. Velsa, what has happened to you?"

Velsa quickly lifted her hand to her face and gasped.

"The heartache from losing you and the pain of hearing of your proposal has done this to me. You have done this to me."

"I never meant to hurt you. I waited for the sign, but it never came. I waited long after my brother told me to end it. It wasn't meant to be."

Velsa could feel her resolve weakening as she tried to hold back the tears that she had sworn she would never shed again. Straightening her back, she glared at him.

"I will ask again, what has brought you to my cottage?"

Gautier began to pace back and forth as if he were rehearsing his words. Finally, he faced her and was shocked at the hatred that stared back at him.

"I fear your hatred for me will cause you to do unthinkable things. I have come to ask you to reconsider the thoughts of revenge that swirl in your mind. If I must, I will beg you to stop if begging will reduce your fury. You must refrain from these unthinkable acts. If it would keep you from this madness, I am prepared to sacrifice myself to save everyone else."

Shrill laughter was all that Gautier heard.

"You are willing to die to save them . . . to save her?"

"If that is what is required."

"Go back to your white wolf. I must think. I can't think when you are around me."

Hanging his head, Gautier took a deep breath and turned to leave.

"Wait, I have one more question to ask of you."

He stopped and looked back at the woman he no longer knew.

"Did you ever love me? Did you ever truly love me?"

Gautier closed his eyes and shook his head.

"No, my affection for you was never love."

Velsa could feel her body shiver, and a sudden pain tore at her heart.

"Leave me," she screamed, as sparks flew from her fingers.

Gautier ran for the shelter of the trees. He could feel the air cool and the light breeze change to a swirling wind. Dark clouds began to gather and lightning crackled around him as he grabbed the reins of his unsteady horse. Mounting him as quickly as he could, his horse raced for Black Thistle without the slightest encouragement.

* * *

Upon his return to Black Thistle, Gautier contacted Godwine to request a meeting of the council. As Gautier entered the Council Chamber, he noticed everyone was present except Astra. A sense of dread filled his thoughts, but he knew waiting on her arrival would be too much of a delay.

"Gautier, please tell the council what you have told me," ordered Gerwig as he reached for Petula's hand.

Gautier stood and began pacing behind Reginald and Lorcan who had been seated on either side of him.

"Recently, Astra brought disturbing news to Lord Heinrich and myself. As members of this council, you all realize how important her visions are to us," declared Gautier.

"We all know the little witch's importance to this council. What did she see?" asked Godwine.

"She brought news of a curse that will be cast upon the Wispet Canyon. The canyon will be filled with flames and everything within it will die. Our beloved Wispets will be driven from the canyon. Astra met with the Wispet Queen, and she is preparing her people for an escape through her portal. The queen is cautious, and I assume they have already left."

"Who is to blame for this curse?" asked Reginald.

"Who is to blame? I am to blame, but there is more," Gautier winced, as the men pounded their fists upon the table and shouted their obscenities at him.

"Astra has also seen a war coming to this castle. Unfortunately, it is a war that we will not win. Our castle will be demolished. A war between witches will cause many innocents to die."

Everyone turned and looked at Derora, and Godwine stood so suddenly he knocked his chair to the floor as he reached for the witch. Gautier grabbed Godwine's arm and pulled him back.

"It is not Derora. She has always been faithful to Black Thistle and its people. Your quarrel is with Velsa. Astra has seen Velsa offer the curse against the Wispet Canyon and demolish our castle."

Several members of the council shouted, "Why?"

"Sadly, this is where I am to blame. It is to avenge my rejection of her affection. I have taken Kayleigh as my mate, and Velsa is devastated. She feels betrayed."

"This is ridiculous," shouted Godwine. "All of this worry is because of a scorned woman. Talk to the woman and make her see reason.

"I have tried. I fear I have made it worse."

"Do you honestly believe that she is capable of what you have told us?" asked Godwine.

Gautier shook his head, "I can't be sure. One moment she speaks calmly, and the next moment, her words are filled with hatred."

"She has let the darkness claim her, and it will help her. Truth-be-told, it will influence her and tempt her to do those horrible things," explained Derora. "Once the darkness has tasted your blood, it owns you. Your desires are no longer your own. With each spell she casts with dark magic, she becomes stronger. I, alone, could not fight a witch that practices black magic."

"There are other witches on the island. Will they come to our aide?" asked Reginald.

"Ingrid and Iris of Cumberland Castle would willingly help me fight the witch. Ida would too, but she is too young. She should stay at Evergreen Castle and try to protect Lord and Lady Evergreen if the war should spread," she replied.

Gerwig stood and the chamber quieted, waiting for him to speak.

"Naturally, I am worried for the people of the castle. All precautions should be taken to protect them. I will stand alongside you to fight this scorned witch, but I must send Petula back to Featherstone. I swore to her father that I would protect her."

"No, I won't leave you," cried Petula. "My place is with you and our people."

"Hush, my love. I am bound by my word to protect you."

Gerwig leaned over and placed his hands upon the table as he made eye contact with each member of his council.

"Reginald, I will rely on you as my commander to come up with a plan to defend Black Thistle from an attack. If we are attacked and the moment becomes bleak, I put Petula and her maids in your charge. I order you to get them safely through the tunnels to Evergreen Forest and eventually back to Featherstone. If I survive, I will join them later," ordered Gerwig.

"Yes, My Lord," replied Reginald.

"Lorcan and Hugh, I order you to stand watch at the Wispet Canyon. If Velsa comes near the canyon, we need to know it."

"Yes, My Lord," they replied.

"Derora, can your magic offer us a warning if Velsa is near?"

"I can and I will, My Lord," replied Derora.

"Gautier, I will expect you to fight along with the witches to protect this castle. Your magic would offer us more protection than your sword."

"As you wish, My Lord," replied Gautier.

"Now, let's not worry our people over this. If Velsa calms down, we are all better for it. If Lorcan and Hugh bring us news of the curse, we will ready ourselves with Reginald's plan. Until then, we must stay vigilant. If the day comes that I must leave this world with a war around me, I could not be prouder than to leave it with all of you. Your trust in me, your faithfulness to our people, your blade of protection, and your bravery have never wavered."

Gerwig stepped back away from the table and drew his fist over his heart as he bowed his head to honor the members of his council. Chairs scraped against the stone floor as each member stood and fisted their chest.

"For Honor and Black Thistle," everyone shouted. "For Honor and Black Thistle."

Chapter 13

Gautier stepped from his bedchamber out onto the balcony. He could feel the cold stone beneath his bare feet and the chill of the breeze against his face. The warm weather had released its hold on the land and stepped aside for the beginning of the cold season. As he looked down at the ladders that pierced the tunnels, he hoped that Velsa had also stepped aside to allow her thoughts of revenge to fade away.

A sudden warmth pressed against his back as Kayleigh's arms wrapped around his waist. He could feel her rest her head against his back, and he took comfort in her touch.

"Do you think she has forgotten? Do you think we are all safe?" she asked.

Gautier turned within her arms so that he could face her.

"Two full moons have passed since I last faced her. It has been much too quiet."

"Come back to bed with me. Let's take advantage of the quiet."

Gautier took in her smile that brightened her eyes and leaned in to capture her mouth with his own. Before their lips could touch, the sound of ringing bells announced Derora's warning.

"Velsa is coming," he muttered.

As he began to force Kayleigh back into their bedchamber, he caught sight of Velsa standing outside the gate.

"Gautier, I want Gautier," screamed Velsa. "Let me see Gautier."

"Don't go; please don't go," whispered Kayleigh.

"You have my attention, Velsa. What do you want?" Gautier shouted, as he kept his arms wrapped tightly around Kayleigh.

He could see the army leading women and children to the tunnels, and he watched as mothers handed their babes down to waiting arms that would carry them to safety.

"I have thought more about this predicament that has separated us. There is a simple solution that will make both of us happy," shouted Velsa.

"And, what is this solution that you offer?" he replied.

"Come with me. Leave the mongrel and take me as your mate. It will save all that Astra has shown you. Think about it. We are evenly matched. A witch and a warlock are a perfect pair. Let the mongrel find her own kind."

"My stars, the woman is crazy," cried Kayleigh.

Gautier waited to answer. He could see her pacing outside the gate, but he wanted to give the army more time to assist the good people of the castle.

"I did not think it would be such a difficult decision. I need your answer, Gautier. I will not wait much longer."

"I made a vow to Kayleigh, and I will not break it. I will never take you as my mate. If it is your plan to provide me with my death, I will die as the mate of my beloved Kayleigh."

Furious over his denial and the sight of their loving embrace, Velsa raised her arms in fury. The air around her took on a purple hue as it swirled around her head. A jeweled dagger appeared, and she drew it across her palm. As the blood dripped to the ground, she began to chant.

Thistles turning black
 Die upon their stalks
Thistles live again
 To sing within the dark

171

Thistles one desire
    To sup upon your blood
Thistles standing tall
    Thriving on my hatred
I demand it now
    Today and forever

The thistles twisted in pain, and their shrieks of agony filled the air. As each purple bloom shriveled and died, their green stalks turned black, and their thorns grew twice as long. Velsa smiled as she walked through the patch of shivering thistles. Holding her bleeding hand above each shriveled bloom, she carefully allowed one drop of blood to fall, and they lovingly scraped their thorns against her hand in appreciation.

Kayleigh looked away and felt Gautier press a kiss to the top of her head.

"Take me inside," she said, as she struggled to remove what she had seen from her mind.

Gautier lifted Kayleigh up into his arms letting her rest her head against his shoulder. He looked one last time at Velsa and made his way into their bedchamber.

Velsa noticed Gautier no longer stood upon his balcony, but she was sure he had seen what she had done.

"Gautier, know that this is all your fault. In return for your denial, I will unleash my wrath against you and all you hold dear," she screamed.

She turned her back on Black Thistle Castle, raised her arms, and vanished.

* * *

"My Lady, you must leave. The women and children have made their way through the tunnels and have arrived safely in the Evergreen Forest. It is time for you to do the same," declared Reginald. "If you wait much longer, it may be too late."

"Go, my love. I will find you when I am able," whispered Gerwig. He kissed Petula one last time and watched as Reginald pulled her fingers from the sleeve of his tunic.

As they reached the open door, Petula fainted, and Reginald lifted her limp body up into his arms.

"Take care of her. Keep her safe for me," begged Gerwig.

Reginald nodded and swept Petula away before he could change his mind.

Only a moment passed before Gautier charged into his chamber.

"Hugh and Lorcan have returned. The witch is at the canyon," he barked. "You are needed in the Great Hall. Derora and the witches from Cumberland Castle are waiting for you."

Without hesitation, he ran after his brother.

* * *

Velsa appeared at the edge of Wispet Canyon. She looked down at the rows of lush lavender and the tiny stone cottages that filled the canyon floor. It was all so beautiful. As she stood admiring the beauty, a memory slowly crept into her mind, and she waited to see it unfold.

Gautier spread a soft linen blanket under a tree covered with pink blooms. She remembered he had chosen the spot to protect her fair skin from the sun. The smell of lavender filled the air, and she could hear birds singing a sweet melody. Gautier leaned back against the tree and beckoned her to sit with him. She knelt down between his legs and leaned back against his chest. His breath was warm against her neck, and she thought this would be the moment the heat would come. As he touched her arm, she waited for the rush of heat, but it didn't come.

"The heat never came," she mumbled. "The heat never came."

173

Velsa doubled over and felt pain tear at her soul. Forcing herself to stand, she raised both of her arms and faced the canyon. Purple balls of light filled her hands, and she began to chant.

Bring forth the hail and lightning

Bring forth the wind and fire

Demolish its purple beauty,

    that brought happiness and love

Take away all gifts of power

Take away the need for life

Let them dwell in utter obscurity,

    full of hatred and full of spite

The white fluffy clouds that always lingered over the canyon began to turn dark. A fierce wind began to swirl through the floor of the canyon tearing the thatching from the roofs of the stone cottages. Hail the size of figs encased in fire fell from the clouds, and Velsa watched as the rows of lavender caught fire, and one cottage after another crumbled to the ground. The stone path that offered a safe descent to the canyon's floor shattered as the stones separated and fell away from the ragged cliff. Steam billowed up from boiling streams and the waterfalls ran dry.

When Velsa turned to leave the canyon, it was clear that every living thing had died. The ground was black from the fires that continued to burn.

"The Wispet Canyon is no more," she snickered. "This dark hole in the ground will be known forever as the Canyon of Obscurity. Darkness, are you pleased with me?"

She felt a warm embrace as she vanished back to her cottage to rest.

* * *

The witches and Kayleigh were huddled together in the Great Hall waiting for Lord Heinrich. As Gautier and his brother entered through one door, Lorcan and Hugh entered through the other.

"Tell me what you have seen," demanded Gerwig. "Has she done it?"

"We saw her step to the edge of the canyon, My Lord. We left as the wind began to blow," replied Hugh. "We could smell the smoke as we rode away."

"What of the Wispet Queen, has she gone?" asked Gautier.

"The canyon was empty when we arrived. The Wispet Queen and her people have left through the portal. She has closed it, for there was no sign of the shimmering orb within the canyon," offered Lorcan. "I fear it won't be long before Velsa is at the gate."

"The women and children have escaped through the tunnels, and I saw Petula and her maids escorted by Reginald down the ladders," said Kayleigh.

"Then, all that remains are the army, our witches, a few brave men that volunteered to fight, and us," laughed Gerwig. "A meager army to fight a witch with the power of the darkness by her side."

"Iris, Ingrid, and I will stand at the gate. We'll be the first targets. She'll want to break the barrier and take our power. If we go down, her strength will multiple tenfold," explained Derora. "Gautier, try to stay hidden, but I will need to draw on your power to keep her back. Know that it will weaken you. If I do not survive, you may be left helpless against Velsa's attack."

"Take what you need from me. It will be our only hope," he replied.

"What can I do?" asked Kayleigh.

"Stay hidden," snapped Derora. "Velsa will be searching for you. If she finds you it could be your end."

"If she gets close to me, I'll bite her head off," smirked Kayleigh.

Gautier laughed. He knew she could do it.

"Take your positions," ordered Gerwig. "She is probably on her way."

* * *

Velsa screamed Gautier's name, and it slammed into the barrier. The force of it caused a few decorative stones to fall from the outer wall.

"Velsa, we know of your curse against the Wispet Canyon. You should be ashamed," shouted Derora. "We can hear the tears of your mother. She is saddened by your behavior."

Velsa floated up above the gate so that she could see those that stood against her.

"Derora, step aside. There is no need for you to be hurt. My quarrel is with the man that betrayed me. I see even now that he lacks the courage to face me."

"If your quarrel is with Gautier, your quarrel is with all of us."

"My dear sweet Derora, do you really want to challenge me? You know who stands beside me. He is much more powerful than the both of us put together. You have little chance of surviving this fight. Walk away and I will forget that you stood against me."

Iris and Ingrid stepped from the shadows and reached for Derora's hands.

"What is this? You have brought the twins into this fight. You know if I kill one of them, the other one will die too? Send them back to Cumberland Castle where they belong. They are nothing more than a hindrance to me."

"Never," shouted Iris.

"You are nothing more than brave little bookends, as well as, thorns in my backside. You had your chance to survive. Now, shall we begin?" smirked Velsa.

Feeling the darkness wrap his arms around her, Velsa's hands began to fill with bright balls of orange light. She drew back her arm and threw the first blast toward the barrier that protected the main gate. She followed it immediately with another. The barrier shimmered, but it held true. As she raised her arm again, a single row of archers stepped forward from the shadows and knelt on one knee facing Velsa. They drew back their bow and waited for the two men carrying torches to light the tips of their arrows.

"You want to play with fire. I'll give you fire," she screamed, as she hurled the ball of light toward the meadow. The moment it touched the ground, the meadow burst into flames.

Iris let go of Derora's hand and pointed at the clouds until rain began to fall. Slowly the flames died out, and she took hold of Derora's hand again.

Not to be denied, Velsa pressed her hands together and raised them over her head. As she pulled her palms away from each other, the clouds drifted away until there wasn't a cloud in sight. Filling her hands with flames, she hurled them at the meadow. Flames leaped from the ground and smoke filled the air.

Waving her hand over the patch of blackened thistles, she laughed as each one spit a thick black liquid into the water of the moat that surrounded the castle. Soon the moat began to bubble, and green noxious fumes drifted into the air. Pleased with herself, Velsa spun around in circles causing the fumes to form thorny tendrils that slithered up the stone wall reaching for the invisible barrier.

"Attack," screamed Velsa.

Hearing her command, the thorns began to prick the barrier and release their poison. Tiny sparks fought back against the poison and caused some of the thorns to turn black and fall from their host. As a dead thorn fell, a new thorn appeared. Soon, small holes appeared throughout the barrier. The small holes became larger holes until the barrier was gone, and the thorny tendrils spilled over the wall.

The men with torches quickly ran the line of archers, lighting each and every arrow. Aiming at their target, they released their arrows all at once. Cries of pain filled the air as the arrows pierced the tendrils causing them to explode and send balls of fire toward the castle. The men drew more arrows from their quivers and prepared to strike again. As the cries subsided and the smoke cleared, everyone could see that the tendrils had vanished.

The witches quickly raised their arms to build a new barrier, but Velsa had already penetrated the outer wall. The archers raised their bows toward her. She spread her arms wide and waited for their attack. As the arrows flew toward her, she waved them away as if they were nothing.

Derora pulled her hands free and rose up into the air to face Velsa. Her hands pulsed with flames as she stared at the hideous witch.

"What have you done to yourself, Velsa? You have turned into an ugly old hag. Was the darkness worth what it has done to you?" asked Derora.

"Gautier left me with a broken heart, and the darkness has healed it."

"The darkness may have healed your broken heart, but your face is covered with weeping sores. I can smell your rancid breath from here. Does he not care enough about you to heal your body?"

Velsa lifted her hand to the side of her face.

"Ignore the witch. My dear, you are here for a reason. Take what is yours. I won't let you fail," the darkness whispered in her ear. *"Attack her."*

Responding to his will, Velsa threw a ball of yellow light directly at Derora. She watched as Derora turned her head and repelled it with her forearms sending it back at her. Easily deflecting it, Velsa opened her mouth, and red wasps flew from her throat. Unable to defend herself from their stingers, Derora slowly drifted toward the ground. Seeing her distress, Ingrid quickly froze the wasps and encased Derora in a protective bubble. Seeing the meddling witch had come to Derora's aide, Velsa threw a burning dagger at Ingrid's heart. Iris' quick reaction saved her sister by sending the dagger to the ground.

Derora quickly healed herself and burst from the protection Ingrid had provided her. Noticing Velsa's distraction with Ingrid, a web filled with poisonous spiders flew from her hand toward Velsa. As the sticky web clung to Velsa's body, the spiders dripped venom from their fangs. Each drop of poisonous venom that touched Velsa's skin made her scream; however, it was the darkness that brushed them all away.

"Enough of this foolishness," screamed Velsa. "Gautier, where are you? Are you hiding with your little white mongrel?"

Furious over his silence, she flicked her wrist and large stones that secured the tower began to crack. One after another began to fall. Iris tried to secure them, but Velsa flung her toward the outer wall. Ingrid watched her limp body fall to the ground and felt her heartbeat slow. Thinking only of her sister, she let her guard down and hurried to her side. With the twins out of the way, Velsa focused back on the castle.

Velsa stiffened her arms with her clenched fists toward the ground. As she flicked her wrists back and forth, stones exploded from the castle and fell on the army below. Derora turned to see a balcony fall and its door shatter. Knowing she was helpless to fight Velsa with the darkness by her side, she flew toward Velsa and grabbed her around the waist. She pulled on Velsa's magic trying to strengthen her own. Along with her magic came the power of the darkness, and she could feel it fighting her. The more she tried to defeat it, the weaker she felt. It wasn't long before the darkness was helping Velsa pull her own magic away from her. Derora could sense the moment the last of her magic left her body, and she fell lifeless to the ground.

Feeling energized, Velsa threw balls of fire toward the castle and watched as the wooden beams of the roof began to burn. The flames rose higher and higher, and she knew that Gautier and Kayleigh would have to make their escape. When they did, she would end them.

Out of the corner of her eye, she saw Ingrid holding Iris' limp body as she flew away. Not wanting to allow their escape, she followed them to the mountains behind Cumberland Castle. Seeing the witches huddled among the trees, she set fire to the forest and watched as it burned. She could hear the witches' cries for mercy, and she covered her ears with her hands. Not wanting to see anymore, she left them dying on the mountain. As she reached the castle wall, she heard rain falling from a cloudless sky. The fire had been put out and replaced by flowing waterfalls that ran from the top of the mountain where she had last seen them.

Erasing the vision from her mind, she scanned the courtyard for Gautier or Kayleigh. Seeing nothing but Derora's dead body and the burned out ruins of Black Thistle, she flew to the steps to start her search for the man that betrayed her.

***

"Gerwig, you must leave. It appears Velsa has abandoned her fight for the moment. You must know that the end is near, and you won't survive if you stay. The castle is lost. You must go," urged Gautier.

Looking at Kayleigh, he saw her shake her head. "Kayleigh, go with my brother. You must save yourself. If I somehow survive this, I will find you."

"I won't go without you. If death must take us, it will take us together," she stubbornly declared.

"Then, I can't leave you two to suffer alone," Gerwig replied. "I am Lord of this castle. It is my duty to fight until the end."

"Go, find Petula. She loves you. Don't make her live alone. Go to her," begged Gautier. "There is little time but enough to make it through the tunnel."

Gautier didn't wait for his brother to offer another excuse. He grabbed him by the arm and forced him toward the tunnel. As his brother reached the bottom of the ladder, he dropped a lighted torch so he could find his way.

"Remember us, Gerwig. Name your first born after us. Now, run as fast as you can."

He waited until the tunnel went dark and ran to find Kayleigh.

* * *

The people of Black Thistle sat as quietly as they could in the shadows of the Evergreen Forest. Reginald stood over Petula as she knelt by the open tunnel waiting for Gerwig to appear. With every terrifying blast that shook the ground, Petula could hear the echo of dirt and rocks falling inside the tunnel. She feared if Gerwig was on his way, he would surely be killed by the next blast that would cause the weakened tunnel to collapse.

"We need to get your people to safety, My Lady," begged Reginald. "I can smell the smoke that comes from the meadow. If it jumps to the trees, none of us will survive."

Petula looked at the women clutching their children to their breasts and reached for Reginald to help her stand.

"Lord Evergreen has offered my people protection. We must get them to the castle as quickly as we can. Lead them out, and I will follow from behind."

"My Lady, I cannot leave you. I promised to keep you safe," cautioned Reginald.

"Must I order you? Obey me, Reginald. Lead my people to Evergreen," she demanded.

Reginald hesitated, but fisted his chest and ran toward the clearing. As he beckoned the women to stand and follow him, they willingly obeyed, and Petula encouraged many others to follow his lead.

Since they were well on their way, she lifted the black cord from her neck. Finding a boulder, she fell to her knees and crushed the red stone.

"Krega, I need you. Krega, come find me. There is danger," she whispered.

Knowing he would come for her, she hurried to help Reginald get her people to safety.

* * *

Krega stood on the ledge of the sanctuary. The breeze that he had come for had stilled. The air about him was completely quiet. Knowing something was wrong, he scanned the sky and sea for danger. It was the hint of a whisper that caught his attention, and he strained to make sense of it. He held his hand cupped to his ear as he heard her words.

Krega, I need you.
Krega, come find me. There is danger.

Immediately, he jumped into the air and shifted into his griffin as he called out for Cadfan and Henwas to follow him. Krega was beyond the boarder of Crownnail by the time they were both in the air. Hearing of Lady Petula's cry for help, they followed behind their commander toward Alltree Island not knowing what they would find.

Krega was the first to see the smoke rising from the mountains, and he ordered Henwas to see if anyone was in need of help. As Henwas turned toward the mountains, Krega searched for the pulse of the talon that hung around Petula's neck. It wasn't long before he spotted the beacon within a large forest. He could see a stream of people running from the trees toward stone towers. Swooping down, he landed in the clearing and Cadfan behind him. Shifting into their human form, they both ran for the trees.

"Cadfan," yelled Petula. "I'm over here."

Cadfan raced to her side.

"There is a war at Black Thistle, and I believe Gerwig is still within its walls," she cried. "We need to help him."

She looked up to see Henwas circling overhead.

"Take my maids to safety. I need to check the tunnel for Gerwig, one more time before we go."

Cadfan called to Ella and Annalee, as Petula ran for the tunnel. She could hear Krega ordering her to stop, but she kept running. The smoke was beginning to filter through the trees, and she covered her nose and mouth with the hem of her skirt. Reaching the tunnel, she knelt down and called Gerwig's name. She could only hear the blasts and the dirt echoing in the tunnel.

"Come," Krega demanded, as he took hold of her arm to make her stand.

"No, Gerwig may be in the tunnel. I can't leave him," she shouted and pulled her arm away from his grasp.

"Commander, we need to leave. The forest has started to burn," Henwas shouted.

Another blast rocked the ground, and Petula screamed as she heard what she thought was the tunnel collapsing.

"It is time to go," Krega whispered, as he knelt down beside her. "The forest isn't safe."

"I can't leave him, Krega. I can't leave him."

"Henwas, tell Cadfan to help the Commander Reginald get these people to safety. Once you have, take the maids to the harbor. We'll board them on the first ship ready to sail. Do not leave them unattended," Krega ordered. "We'll meet you shortly."

Tears streamed down Petula's face as Krega wrapped his arm around her shoulder. Blast after blast shook the ground, and she could hear more dirt fall in the tunnel. Fearing the fire and smoke would do her harm, he took her arm and lifted her up into his arms. He turned and headed for the clearing. As they stepped from the shade of the trees, Petula heard Gerwig shouting her name.

"Put me down," cried Petula, as she struggled to be set free.

Krega turned to see Gerwig running toward them. His face was covered in dirt and soot, but he was alive.

Once she was on her feet, she ran toward Gerwig. He wrapped his arms around her and thanked the stars for letting him see her again.

"We need to leave," shouted Krega. "We need to leave, now!"

Gerwig took her hand, and they ran for the clearing. He could see Reginald and the Evergreen Army leading his people inside the walls of the Evergreen Castle.

"Krega, can we take my commander with us?" asked Gerwig. "I fear there is nothing left of the army at Black Thistle. He is an honorable man. He would serve Lord Larchmont well."

"We'll see that he is aboard the ship when it sails," replied Krega. "For now, let's get you two to safety."

"What of Gautier and Kayleigh?" asked Petula.

"Gautier saw me safely to the tunnels, but he could not persuade Kayleigh to leave him. I am sure they are at Velsa's mercy by now," he said, as he choked back tears. "He forced me to leave so that you would not be alone."

"Gautier and Kayleigh will always live within our hearts. We will never forget them," whispered Petula, as she wiped the tears from Gerwig's face.

* * *

The smoke was thick, and Gautier led Kayleigh out onto the balcony in hopes of breathing fresh air. With nothing left of his magic, there was nothing else he could do. What they could see through the smoke was devastating. The walls about the castle lay in ruins, and the peoples' cottages were engulfed in flames. The meadow between the castle and the Evergreen Forest was charred as far as they could see. Off in the distance the mountains above Cumberland Castle smoldered. It was unlike anything they had ever seen.

"Is this the end of us?" asked Kayleigh.

Before he could answer, the bedchamber door flew from its hinges and smashed against the wall. Velsa stood in the doorway holding a small black chest.

"Isn't this sweet? The lovebirds are huddled in their nest but unable to fly."

"Haven't you done enough? You've ruined Wispet Canyon and Black Thistle Castle. The earth is black as far as I can see," blurted Gautier. "Who knows how many people have died today."

"Have I done enough? Have I done enough, you ask? That depends on you. I will give you one more chance to end it. Release the mongrel's hand and take mine. Be done with her. Come to me, and I will not harm her. I will send her away some place safe. She can live out her days and let her wolf run free."

Gautier looked down at Kayleigh. He had vowed to protect her, and Velsa was giving him a chance to keep her safe. He knew he couldn't bear to live without her. He would die one day at a time until he finally took his own life to stop the pain. Seeing Kayleigh shaking her head, he glared back at Velsa.

"I will stay with the woman I love until the end. If the end comes today, I will be content knowing that she has loved me, and I have loved her."

"You are fools," she shouted. "You are both fools."

Kicking a chair out of her way, she set the chest down on a small table. After opening it, she withdrew her jeweled dagger and drew it across her palm.

Gautier and Kayleigh kissed one last time and wrapped their arms around each other.

"Look at me, Kayleigh. Don't look away," he begged. "I want your eyes to be the last thing that I see."

Locked in each other's arms, they waited for the end.

Red smoke surrounded Velsa as she lifted her arms and began to chant.

Darkness, Darkness come to me

Take these souls and make them three

Take her swiftly to the dungeon

Keep him hidden in the dark

Let the white wolf always wander

Never touching, always apart

Gautier could feel the bright purple ball of light coming toward them, and he turned to shield Kayleigh from the blast. Pain raced through their bodies as they whispered their last words of love to one another, and then they were gone.

Velsa wiped the blood from her dagger with the hem of her skirt and placed it back in the chest. Pulling a folded parchment from her pocket, she set it carefully on top of the dagger, closed the lid, and secured the latch. Making her way to the wall beside the hearth, she raised her arm and made a fist. As she opened her hand, a wall swung open to reveal a hidden chamber. She walked slowly toward a pedestal that sat in the corner of the dark chamber and placed the chest down on its surface. Leaning over, she kissed the top of the chest and silently whispered Gautier's name. With the wave of her hand, the panel closed, and she felt the darkness take her hand.

"It didn't have to be this way," she muttered. "Now, she is lost to you. Now, you are lost to me. It is a sad ending. An ending that should have been so much different if you . . . if you would have loved me instead. Now, it has ended for all of us."

She reached toward the chest but vanished before her fingers could open the latch.

* * *

When Kayleigh opened her eyes, she found herself cuffed and chained to a dungeon wall. Her body was nothing more than a pale grey vapor that seemed to be fading quickly. Standing at her feet was the image of her wolf.

"Go, save yourself," she choked through the tears. "There is nothing you can do to help me. I am lost."

Her wolf padded toward the door but stopped. Not wanting to leave Kayleigh, she turned back to find she had already vanished. Afraid of what had taken Kayleigh, she leapt through the doorway into a dark fog.

Gautier, can you hear me?

Silence was her only reply.

Gautier, can you hear me?

A painful silence brought tears to her eyes.

Gautier, she may have separated us, but my love for you will last forever.

Gautier had seen the bright light just before he was thrust into a world of darkness. It made no difference if his eyes were open or closed, he couldn't see or feel anything. There was no light from the moon, the stars, or even the flicker of a flame from a single candle to help him. He stood blind, helpless, and alone.

The sudden sound of her voice took his breath away. Holding out his arms, he searched for her.

I can hear you, Kayleigh. Can you hear me?

Again, he heard her call out to him. He realized then that he could hear her but she couldn't hear him.

"Even now, Velsa twists the knife to cause us pain," he sighed.

Tears filled his eyes as he heard her attempt to reach him.

Kayleigh, our love will last forever. I promise you that we will be together again. I will always love you.

Every day Kayleigh called for him, and every day she heard nothing but silence.

Every day Gautier waited to hear her voice. It was the only comfort he had as he sat alone in the darkness and waited for a loophole to break the curse.

* * *

After leaving the hidden chamber, Velsa had spent several days sitting alone in the dark. She had thought of nothing but the day she had met Gautier and played it over and over in her mind. It was Balgair's rap at the door that had caused her to step away from her sweet memories and back into the sadness of the real world.

"What brings you to my cottage? Have I forgotten to make you a potion?" she asked. "Tell me what you want and I can conjure it quite quickly."

"I have just concluded a long voyage and brought you a present," Balgair replied.

"A present, you have brought me a present. I can't remember the last time I was given a present." She smiled and pushed the stray hairs from her face as she stood to greet him. "Show me what you have brought me."

Balgair untied the binding and let it fall to the floor. He watched her eyes brighten as he unfolded the linen to reveal a hand-painted fan.

"It's beautiful, Balgair," she cried. "Where did you find such a thing of beauty?"

"Someplace very far away," he smiled.

She ran her gnarled finger over the flowers that had been painted on the softest silk fabric. The colors reminded her of the wildflowers that grew in the meadow. Remembering what she had done to the meadow, she pulled her hand back fearing she would damage the delicate fan.

"Shall we have a cup of sweet berry wine?" she asked, as she turned to grab her pitcher.

Balgair nodded as he closed the fan and laid it upon the table. He had heard the talk of the War of the Witches when he had stopped at the tavern in Echo Bluff, and the pain of it was still on her face. Taking the cup she had offered him, he raised it high in the air.

"What good cause shall we drink of today?" he asked.

Velsa chewed on her bottom lip as she poured her own cup of wine and then raised her cup to meet his.

"We shall drink to painted fans, visitors, and beautiful memories," she declared. "For, I have since locked all my sadness far away."

Chapter 14

Over two-hundred years had passed since Gautier and Kayleigh had been cursed by the witch named Velsa. During that time, a wicked vampire named Magna had claimed the ruins of Black Thistle Castle and lived deep below the crumbled stones in its dungeon. As mistress of her domain, she thrived on torture and the blood from humans which was the reason for her banishment from the Evergreen Castle. The ruins kept her safe since it was thought to be haunted by ghosts of those that were killed during the War of the Witches. Those that were brave enough to trespass into the castle never found their way home. This kept the rumors alive and Magna safe from the Evergreen Army.

It was Jario, a traitorous vampire, who was wanted for crimes against Lady Lara that eventually merged with Magna and took control of the castle ruins. In his effort to create a safe haven from arrest, he began to rebuild the castle and an army. It was during this endeavor that he discovered something that would change many lives forever.

* * *

Gautier had heard the sounds of the crumbling walls of Black Thistle Castle for years. He had been driven crazy by the sounds in the beginning, but after years of practice, he had learned to drown them out. Now, they were nothing more than a gentle humming. They were nothing compared to the sound of Kayleigh calling his name every night in the darkness. Her voice offered brief moments of sweet comfort before it disappeared to leave him longing to hear her voice again.

Waiting in silence, he searched for the sweet sound of Kayleigh's voice. For a split second, he found his focus drawn from his dark prison. It wasn't the sound of water dripping onto the stone floor, or the wind howling through the collapsed walls, but the sound of boots that had captured his attention. Hearing it again, he began to hope that someone had found him. The sudden sound of stone grinding against stone and the woeful groan of something heavy caused Gautier to still before a gust of fresh air seemed to rush past him.

"What is this?" an unfamiliar voice asked. "I have stumbled upon a secret chamber. Is this where others sat hidden during the War of the Witches?"

He heard something scrape against the floor just before a dim flicker of light caught his attention. Hearing the boots again, he studied their strides and was sure they were worn by a man. This man was either walking in circles or was restricted in his movements.

"Wait, I heard him speak of a chamber. The witch must have confined me to a chamber," whispered Gautier.

As Gautier listened, every sound became magnified. He heard the man opening and closing what he thought were wooden chests, the man's laughter, and the scraping of his boots against the floor. It was hearing the same woeful groan, something scraping against stone, and the man scurrying away that made him hold his breath.

"Please, don't leave," he cried.

As he waited, the silence was finally broken as he heard the groan again. Relaxing his panicked mind, Gautier listened to every movement the man made. It was the sound of flesh stroking metal, and the man's voice that startled him.

"Fuaim na Cumhacta," spoke the stranger. "I know this language. It means Sound of Power. A simple sword like this must

have been a gift to a young man. It isn't sturdy enough to be a warrior's sword."

Hearing those words, Gautier knew the man was reading from his brother's sword. With the hum of the swords song swirling in the air, he was certain of it. He was in Gerwig's hidden chamber.

Caught in the memories of his brother, he didn't hear the man move to stand before him. It was the sound of something opening above him that caught him by surprise. Gautier suddenly felt the man's hands brush against his soul, as the weight of the dagger that had rested on his chest had been lifted. Afraid to breathe, he heard the rustle of old parchment before the crumbling of the wax that had sealed it for so long. The air around him began to cool, and a moan of relief left his lips before he heard the man speak.

Remove the chain, Unbind the pain, Release the fear, Retrieve Gautier

Gautier could see the torch within the chamber flare wildly, and felt the chamber's temperature drop even more as he leaned back against the stone wall. The man that held the parchment, placed it back into the chest and closed the lid. He watched him quickly press a stone within the stone wall, grab the torch from its bracket, and step from the chamber as the door closed.

Standing in the dark, Gautier inhaled the musty air of the chamber. He was finally free of the witch's curse. Hitting the stone with his fist, he watched the door to the chamber slowly open. Stepping from its darkness, he saw the man that had freed him step back with a look of surprise upon his face.

"I am Gautier, and you have released me from a binding spell," he announced with a raspy voice, as he walked to the center of the bedchamber. He slowly turned and looked about the space that surrounded him. Looking back at the man, he raised his hands as if he were confused. "Where is my beloved?

Where is my Kayleigh?" Hearing no response from the man, fear and then anger crossed Gautier's face as he screamed, "Where is she? What have you done with her?"

The man backed up against the wooden door. At once, Gautier had him by the throat with his feet dangling two feet off the ground. The look on Gautier's face was that of uncontrollable rage.

He looked into the man's eyes and asked again, "Who are you, and where is my Kayleigh? I will tear you limb from limb if you have harmed her."

"My name is Jario, and I do not know the woman that you speak of," he managed to choke out, as Gautier's hands relaxed enough for him to speak. "There are only a few of us in the castle and none by the name you have given."

Gautier pulled his hand back and watched him drop. Jario felt his boots and then his knees hit the floor. He reached for his neck and began rubbing the bruises left behind from Gautier's strong grip. Gautier paced anxiously about the chamber as he continued to stare at Jario. Trying to calm himself, he moved to the window. Gazing out into the darkness, he realized that time had changed all that he remembered. The castle was in ruins, and the War of the Witches had ended.

"Who won the War of the Witches?" Gautier asked, not turning to look at Jario. "It was during the war that a spell was cast upon me, binding me to that chamber."

"The legends, told by many, say that Velsa won the war," Jario coughed, still rubbing his neck. "Were you the Lord of this castle during the war?"

"Velsa?" Gautier repeated the name Jario had used, as he closed his eyes searching his memories. "I remember that old hag. She is not to be trusted, and my binding is proof of it." He paced back and forth in front of the window with his hand held to his brow. "You must forgive me, my memories seem to be muddled and are offering me some pain when I search them. To answer your question, no. This was my brother's castle. He was a human and must have died in the war along with many others. If not then, he has surely passed by now." He stopped and stood still as he gazed out the window. "I lived here in the castle with my beloved, Kayleigh. I fear she is lost to me, as well."

"As you can see, I am trying to repair the castle," Jario said, hoping not to raise fury into Gautier. "I plan to live in this castle and build an army."

Gautier turned and declared, "I owe you a great debt for breaking the binding spell. I have the power to help you restore the castle."

"What power is this?" Jario asked. Unsure of a man wielding power, he took a few steps back toward the door.

"Power beyond anything you can imagine," Gautier smirked, as he waved his hand and made a fire appear within the hearth. "If you have not figured it out, I am a warlock. I have made a few witches angry over the years, Velsa in particular. She has a quick temper and felt scorned by me. She was the reason why I found myself the subject of her binding spell."

Jario listened carefully to his offer of help to restore the castle.

"Is this power something that you can teach me?" asked Jario. "I have need of revenge for an injustice done to me."

"I can relate to the revenge of injustice. I, myself, feel the need for revenge. However, once I know that I can trust you, vampire, we can discuss lessons," Gautier replied, with a smirk. "Yes, I know that you are a vampire. Let's walk outside. I need to feel the night air. It has been quite stuffy where I have been held."

Jario turned and reached for the door. He heard the sound of Gautier's boots close behind him. Grabbing the iron handle, he pulled the door open for Gautier to exit the chamber. As Gautier took a step forward, a terrifying scream was heard echoing through the stone hallways. Gautier turned to look at Jario for an explanation. Frozen in place, he heard his name pierce his ears, and felt the strength of it slam against his chest knocking his feet out from under him.

"The dungeon," shouted Jario. "It must have come from the dungeon."

The two men ran through the hallways and down the flight of stone steps to the dungeon. Stepping into its dim light, Jario saw Magna standing in front of a closed cell door. She turned when she heard them approaching and lifted her hand to point toward the cell.

"She just appeared out of thin air," Magna said, as her voice cracked more from surprise than fear. "She was bound by chains until they fell from her wrists. I have no idea where she came from."

Looking in the direction that Magna pointed, Jario saw a woman standing in the middle of the cell. She was pale and thin with long curly hair the color of flax and wore an ivory dressing gown that was not of the current style. Hearing the movement within the dungeon, the woman looked up and immediately held up her arms.

"Gautier! Oh, my love. You have found me," she cried, as tears ran down her face. "I was alone, and it was so very dark and cold. Gautier, I could not find you."

He rushed to the cell, and with the wave of his hand, the cell door flew open crashing against the iron bars. Pulling her to his body, he felt her rest her face against his chest and the heat of her tears as they streamed down her face. Finally embraced in each other's arms, they let their love melt against each other.

He held her tightly with one arm around her waist as he caressed her hair with his other hand and softly repeated, "Kayleigh! Kayleigh! My sweet Kayleigh."

* * *

Balgair had waited long enough for Velsa to open the door. As he stepped through the stone wall of her cottage, he found her sitting in the dark by a cold hearth. Pressing his fingers together, he created a small flame that he used to bring the candles around the room to flame. With the light, he could see the sorrow in her eyes.

"Velsa, what has you in such a state?" asked Balgair.

"The wind has brought me news that I knew would come one day."

"What news is this?"

"My binding spell has been broken. My only love, Gautier, and his mongrel have been set free. I am sure they are in each other's arms as we speak."

"You had your revenge. They were locked away from each other for a long time."

"It is true. I have had my revenge upon those I felt betrayed me. It is the innocents that suffered that I have come to regret."

"Be satisfied that your broken heart has been avenged."

"Balgair, it all happened so long ago, and the sweetness of that moment no longer lingers in my mind. My dabbling with the darkness has had ramifications on all who dwell on this island. I know of what I speak." Velsa raised her hand to allow her gnarled fingers to touch her face. "I have suffered greatly from my own desires, and one day, those that I have harmed will seek to place their justified revenge upon me. Until that day comes, I will try to survive without Gautier."

"You still have your magic, and it can protect you. I, for one, will always be in need of your magic. We made a bargain I expect you to honor."

"My dear friend, I will honor our bargain, but even with magic, a life without love is an empty life."

"You are not the Velsa that I have known all these years. The Velsa I have known was never afraid to fight for what she wanted. She was bold in her actions, alluring, often sarcastic, spiteful, and clever. They may not be the best traits for a woman, but for a witch, it heightens the mystique."

Balgair watched as Velsa pushed herself up from her chair and turned to face him. As she moved toward him, he saw her raised brow, the hint of a smile, and the tilt of her head. He had seen that look many times before.

"What are you thinking about?" Balgair asked, as he started to back away from her. "Velsa, what are you going to do?"

"Whatever I want, Balgair. Whatever wicked thing I want," she replied, as she vanished into thin air and left Balgair surrounded by a wisp of blue smoke.

Epilogue

It had been a strained adjustment for Gautier, Kayleigh, and her wolf after their release from Velsa's binding spell. Black Thistle Castle stood in ruins, and they were surprised to find vampires had occupied their castle. If that weren't enough, it appeared the new lord of the castle was building an army and preparing for war.

As days passed, they had rarely left each other's side and never truly believed that they had been set free. In their own quiet way, they had mourned the loss of those that had fought by their side, and the certain passing of Gerwig and Petula. It was their hope that one day they would venture to Crownnail Island and find that the people of Featherstone had loved them. Until then, they would live each day to its fullest and cherish every moment they were together.

* * *

Gautier stood on the balcony with Kayleigh safe in his arms. It had been the last place that they were together before their world had been torn apart.

"Do you remember us?" asked Kayleigh. "Do you remember the goodness of us?"

"I remember all of it, my love," replied Gautier, as he kissed the tip of her nose. "I remember the first day I saw you, the first time I saw your wolf, our first kiss, and the day I found you on the Isle of Tears. Do you want me to continue? Do you want to hear more of my memories?"

"Please, it warms my heart to hear what you have remembered about us."

"I remember the day I took you behind the waterfall in the Wispet Canyon, the look upon your face when you agreed to be mine, the day we said our vows, the white petals that led to our marriage bed, how beautiful you looked when your sleeping gown fell to the floor, the feel of your soft skin, and the way you said my name as we became one. I have remembered all of the goodness and the love we shared.

"They are wonderful memories, and I will always cherish them."

"Those memories, as lovely as they are, are only memories. We must never forget how lucky we are to have been given a second chance. We are able to see each other, touch each other, and hear each other's voices. Your white wolf has been returned to you, and she can run free with the moonlight. We must never take those simple pleasures for granted."

"I will never forget, Gautier. We are so very lucky."

He leaned down and captured her mouth with his own. As he did, he remembered the evening he kissed her for the first time. As he pulled back, he saw the same warm flush upon her cheeks and smiled.

"How long will you love me?" asked Kayleigh.

Gautier smiled and brushed his thumb over her flushed cheek.

"Forever," he replied.

"Forever?" she asked.

"My little white wolf, I will always love you."

She rested her face against his chest and felt the comfort of his strong arms wrap around her.

"Always and forever," whispered Kayleigh. "Always and forever."

"Yes, always and forever," he replied.

A Note from the Author

Thank you for reading Trapped Alone. I hope you enjoyed the Prequel to the Evergreen Series. It was fun creating the magical transformation of Velsa and telling the love story of Gautier and Kayleigh. If you have already read the Evergreen Series, I hope it answered those things you were curious about.

Note: Gautier and Kayleigh make their appearance in Book II of the series after being released from Velsa's binding spell. Their story continues on through the rest of the series. Also, you will learn more about Astra and her challenge to survive her banishment to the mountain in Book III and more about her in Book IV.

If you enjoyed this book, please take a moment to leave a review at Amazon, B&N, Goodreads, or your favorite eBook provider. It need not be long or detailed, but I would ask that it be honest.

I would love to hear from my readers. You can reach me at any of the sites below. I will do my best to respond as quickly as I can. I look forward to hearing from you.

Website: www.authorjoannherley.com

Facebook: www.facebook.com/authorjhbooks

Email: info@authorjoannherley.com